I0724610

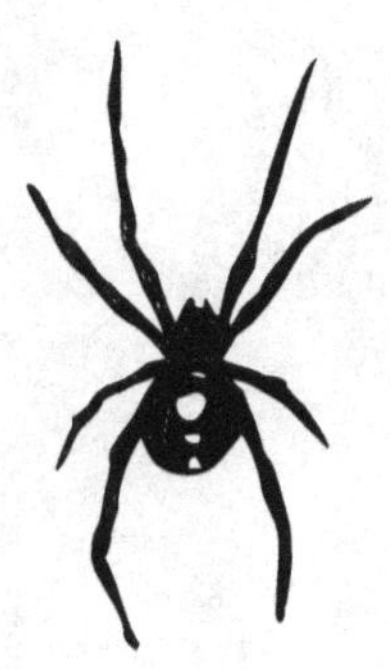

THE HANGMAN FEEDS THE JACKAL

HOTEL

COY HALL

THE HANGMAN FEEDS THE JACKAL

A GOTHIC WESTERN

N•P NOSETOUCH PRESS
CHICAGO | PITTSBURGH

The Hangman Feeds the Jackal

Copyright © 2022 by Coy Hall
All Rights Reserved.

ISBN-13: 978-1-944286-24-8
Paperback Edition

Published by Nosetouch Press
www.nosetouchpress.com

For more information, contact Nosetouch Press:
info@nosetouchpress.com

Cataloging-in-Publication Data

Names: Hall, Coy, author.
Title: The Hangman Feeds the Jackal
Description: Chicago, IL : Nosetouch Press [2022]
Identifiers: ISBN: 9781944286248 (paperback)
Subjects: LCSH: Western stories—Fiction. |
GSAFD: Western stories. | BISAC: FICTION / Westerns.

Cover & Interior Designed by Christine M. Scott
www.clevercrow.com

FOR OLIVIA
AND LOCKSLEY

BEING AN ACCOUNT OF A
MONASTERY IN THE WILDERNESS.

THE FOREST WAS FULL OF ABERRATIONS THAT NIGHT.

When he inched closer to the fissure, his skin touched cool stone, and the contact brought him back to reality. He was dreaming with eyes open again. Elijah Valero shook his head and breathed deeply. Nausea moved through him. He'd watched the road since the first light of morning, he realized.

Through a gash in the wall, the forest road was visible for some distance. The opening was more arrow slit than window, no more than four inches wide at its largest and a hairline at its narrowest, so Valero saw without being seen. The gash was one of many holes in the surrounding walls. Nature worked to reclaim the monastery. The stones were eroding, the wood rotting.

Valero had lost track of time weeks prior. He'd nearly starved himself. His arms were like stray bones in the darkness.

Shame. Shame is good, he reminded. *Shame is a dash of clarity.*

Still, Valero was compelled to remain and watch. He put his eye to the stone again, appreciating the cleverness of his high perch. Although moonlight was faint, he saw for some distance past the crumbling front walls of the garden. The dirt trace, which meandered downward through a pine grove, had been empty since dawn save for a lone coyote that used the road for a hundred yards and wandered into the brush again. Judged by the invasive trees and bramble that flanked the edge and grass that erupted in strips across its width, the path hadn't been used with regularity since Spanish missionaries controlled the region. That was a century prior.

Hills with long valleys stretched in every direction. The red cedars were tall and virginal. Black soil and a mulch of dead leaves covered the hillside. Creatures trampled through the undergrowth each morning, leaving their musk in the air. When the sun was up and the sky was clear, mountains were visible in the distance.

Amid all this stood the monastery, appearing as though the ruins had sprouted like chipped teeth from the hilltop, ensnared by vines.

Civilization kept its distance. At night, despite the chorus of crickets, owls, and nighthawks, the rush of the Kinnikinnick River a mile to the west was audible. Such was the lack of men and their chatter. On clear mornings, the train that passed through Bone-of-Wellington, two hours southward, could be heard. The locomotive ran every two weeks.

Buried in the foothills of the Klamath Mountains, this was a thoroughly desolate corner of the world.

A feminine voice entered Valero's mind. The voice arrived with such clarity that it sounded as though a woman stood at his side, whispering.

Don't become complacent, she warned.

He turned, looking for her in the darkness. Valero's pride sank. She was monitoring him. Not even his thoughts were private.

She urged Valero to maintain his vigil. Her voice broke into layers—a rush of noise that reached a crescendo and then ebbed to a whisper.

Valero was accustomed to her warnings. The Spider (he labeled the voice by the only form he witnessed it assume) was persistent of late. She insisted on Valero's attention. She enraptured him, ravaged him, promised him, and threatened him. She'd left him in this shell to watch the road. He grew tired of her, but, then again, when had he welcomed her presence? The Spider invaded. There was no other way to phrase it. It was not a question of belonging or love. She occupied Valero when she saw fit. She was a sickness.

A swell of guilt bruised Valero.

You should thank her, he thought, *not admonish her*.

At her core, the Spider tried to protect him. Was she overprotective? Perhaps, yes, but when he was unsure of his instinct, she became his intuition.

Watch, she said.

As if an invisible hand guided his chin, Valero returned to the gash in the wall.

She reminded Valero that, no matter his effort to flee and hide, he could never be alone for long, not even in this corner of the world.

Watch and listen.

Keep your vigil.

Elijah Valero was a hounded man, after all. He'd die that way. She knew this as well as he, but, like a mother, she pitied him. She prolonged his existence out of charity. The Spider was wise. She was right more often than wrong.

To Valero's astonishment, a figure moved in the darkness outside. A man, with a violent struggle through the bramble that was heard before seen, rewarded Valero's faith. Valero shifted his gaze, searching. Through a break in the pines, a grey man appeared. The Spider was correct, but the realization brought Valero no delight. Terror moved through him.

The man moved up the trail, making no effort to be silent. He thrashed loudly through tufts of switchgrass in mockery of Valero's concealment. Arrogantly, he walked without a horse, without any possessions at all. He wandered upward like a spirit from the valley.

He comes for one purpose, the Spider said.

The man gripped a stick, with which he beat back the grass, reaping weeds as he came forward. The grass swished with his advance. He had the look of a vagrant, but a benign appearance wouldn't disarm Valero.

In the final stretch before the front gate, the trail was an uphill slog. Once the grey man emerged from the tree line, he stopped for a breather, doubling at the waist. He wiped sweat from his face and neck. The night was muggy. Seized, the man coughed. He hacked for a full minute. He spat shredded lungs on the ground.

The grey man cut a sorry figure. Even from this distance, Valero saw the multitude of scabs on the man's flesh. The clothes he wore looked like rags purloined from a grave. Around his neck he wore a threadbare scarf. On his feet were rotten, ill-fitting boots. He wore no hat to shade the blistered, scabbing face. He had restless, twitching hands that were jaundiced and abnormally long.

The Hangman, the Spider observed. *Do you recognize his specter?*

So it was.

No matter the shape he assumed or the air he affected, the Hangman remained the same. He disarmed first, and then he killed. He beguiled, and then he struck.

Of course, she said, *he'll try to fool you with his appearance. He's done so before. Remember the child?*

He did. Valero's shame retreated beneath the Spider's growing shadow. She had pride even if he did not.

Remember the widow?

Remember the soldier? He, too, in grey?

Be careful lest he beguile you.

Valero agreed. It was the Hangman come again.

After shrinking back from the fissure, Valero groped in the dark for his satchel. Finding the worn leather case, he reached inside and retrieved a Colt Navy, heavy with six bullets.

The grey man moved forward. He sweated profusely. He was a slight man, underfed, grizzled.

Walking bones, Valero thought. *An empty shape sewn together sloppily.* It was as if his body, too, had been filched from graves.

A *phantasm,* the Spider said.

When the grey man passed through the curtain wall, a large entryway shored with pillars of wood, he reached the gardens of the monastery. Here, where once there was an artwork of flowers corniced with decorative stone, squirmed reams of briar, weed, and switchgrass. Paint on the stones had faded, save for smudges of burgundy. The Hangman looked in awe at the towering ruins. Valero's ingenuity struck him.

Valero's heart thudded.

The Hangman's eyes stopped on the second story fissure. His gaze lingered there.

The Hangman whistled in admiration. Despite a century of abandonment, the great building impressed him. The monastery stood black against the sky.

Cloaked in the cell's darkness, Valero clicked the revolver's hammer into place. The cylinder rotated. The aroma of gun oil came to him. The sensation comforted him.

You're worthless, the mercurial Spider nagged. *He heard the gun. He smelled the oil. He looked past you, but he saw your hiding place. Watch his eye linger—Watch. He knows you're here. Why else would he have come? How dare you make such a racket?*

Upon the wall, a black spider scuttled. The creature had no web, and it hadn't been present moments prior. Valero's breath caught. The Spider materialized from the rock, like condensation. Voice became flesh. As Valero watched, the Spider grew. First to the size of a dime and then to the width of a silver dollar. The legs stretched, then the body bloated into proper proportion.

It was a sight of wonder.

Keep watching the garden, she admonished. *You see? He's gone. You lost him. He could be anywhere. He could be in this room. He could be....* She stopped then.

Indeed, the Hangman had gone from the garden. Save for a breeze that cooled the sweat on Valero's face and swayed the treetops, the forest did not move. The road stood empty. The Hangman had not retreated down the path.

He's inside, Valero thought.

The Hangman's proximity disturbed Valero.

For a moment, he was an eight-year-old boy again, looking at the unmoving form of his mother while cowering in the shadow of the Hangman. Valero breathed in, blunting the edge of his terror. Finally, after checking the cell, Valero stood. The bones of his legs creaked. He winced at the noise. After a look at the Spider, crawling with quizzical patience atop his satchel, Valero crept toward a doorway.

The cell in which he practiced his watch was small and confined, a pocket of stone and no more. The corridor into which the door opened was more expansive, stretching twenty feet across and reaching to the high, vaulted ceiling. Any decoration for the hall was long plundered. The space was bare and musty, and it reeked of rat feces and urine. Moss grew on the plank floor. Vines penetrated the ceiling. The air was thick and still.

It remained darker here, with only a few shafts of moonlight lancing the rotten wood above. Light silvered the floor here and there, and where it did rats were visible. Rodents crossed the planks with no interest in Valero or the Hangman. Their only worry was a horned owl perched on a rafter.

As Valero moved through the darkness, he thought once more of his mother. He thought of the Hangman kneeling in front of him atop creek stones. The man gripped a noose. There she was, on the road, her naked feet, blackened and hard. Her body was like snow.

The memory strengthened Valero's rage. He lifted the Colt Navy and moved towards the stairwell.

IN a settlement called Bone-of-Wellington, Felix Hines awoke in a hovel. His head buzzed with the residue of a nightmare. He recalled the anxiety of the dream, but he remembered none of the finer details. Sweat rather than blood covered his body now. His pillow was damp. To his horror, he had urinated through his pants onto the floor. The puddle was cold, stretching to where his sister lay, soaking the fringe of her mat.

In the tall bed, his father and mother slept loudly. If his father awoke to find the mess, he'd ball his fist and strike Felix. Then, after the beating was complete and the sun had risen, father and son would head to the sawmill as if nothing occurred.

With an anguished effort to remain silent, Felix disentangled himself from the mat and blanket, and then he stood in the darkness. The air was hot to the point of suffocation. Treading lightly, he moved to the front door of the single room hovel. He turned a block of wood that held the door. He opened the door, and the hinges groaned.

The street was quiet and dark, flanked by twin rows of wilting shacks. The moon cast its light over the settlement, glazing the edge of the distant sawmill, and painting the Kinnikinnick River blue-white. The only creatures that moved were the tomcats that prowled alleyways and stalked the graveyard in search of mice and moles.

Beyond the shacks, a floodplain met the river. Tall grass covered the expanse, mashed against the mud where horses exercised. Hoofprints pocked the ground. Horse stench lingered, mingling with the astringent chemicals from the mill. Felix's boots sank half an inch with each step, and mud sucked at his feet. He slapped his way through a swarm of mosquitoes.

On a large stone at the riverbank—a stone that had more than fifty names carved into it—sat two familiar shapes. At first, Felix was startled to see he was not alone. One man stripped threads of beef jerky and dropped it down his throat like a vulture with carrion, while the other launched pebbles into the current. The rocks splashed with small puckers. The water gulped with each toss.

Deep in conversation, the men didn't acknowledge Felix as he trampled across the field, approaching. Their voices drifted to Felix. The men argued. Felix recognized the one with the jerky as Corbin Blum and the other man pitching stones as Spence Hickman. Like Felix and his father, like all men in the settlement, Corbin and Spence worked at the mill.

"It wouldn't do just to fuckin' search," Spence was saying.

"Then what?"

"You know what."

Felix made himself conspicuous, clearing his throat when the men were within earshot.

The argument ceased.

Corbin nodded.

"Evenin', Felix," he said.

Spence kept his massive back turned.

"Evenin'," Felix said.

Felix knew Corbin and Spence, although not well. The men were drifters, and they'd been at the mill for only a couple weeks. They were, as Felix understood it, working to earn travel money. He had a few drinks with them one night at Rand's Hotel, and the duo regaled him with some gruesome tales.

Felix walked up to the stone. Years before, he carved his name into the surface. It was there in the chicken scratch of signatures.

"Could be you could help us out," Corbin said. He was a tall man, gaunt, with a withered eye in the left socket. He wore no patch over that ocular monstrosity. "Spence says you're a brain."

Spence kept his face to the river. He wrapped his fingers around the pebbles in his hand as if they were jewels.

Felix shook his head in disagreement. Being able to read made a man a scholar in Bone-of-Wellington, though.

It was then that Corbin broached the subject of Old Man Argo's silver for the first time. It would not be the last. The subject was, Felix came to find, an obsession for Corbin Blum.

Felix listened, fascinated.

"From what I gather there's goddamn $50,000 worth of silver bullion and coins," Corbin went on. "Whatta you know 'bout it?"

"Only the same stories everybody knows," Felix said.

"How much you fuckin' believe it?" Corbin asked.

Felix shrugged. He didn't really believe it, but he kept that to himself.

"Well, I want it," Corbin said. He believed. That was what was important. "There's an idea percolating in Spence's head over there. He's a brain, too, ya know."

Spence finally talked. "Kid, your old man's a fuckin' bastard, ain't he?"

"Yeah," Felix muttered.

"What would you do to your old man if there were no consequences? I mean nothin' at all would happen to you. You'd do it and that's it."

Feeling transparent, Felix asked, "What's that have to do with Old Man Argo's silver?"

Spence was silent.

"The idea's percolatin'," Corbin said. "You watch." He winked his single eye. "I'm gonna guess just about everything. How 'bout it, Felix? Out with it, you crazy fucker."

Leaning against the stone, Felix told them what he'd like to do to his father. The words came in a rush.

The detail was careful, even if the words were not.

THE monastery was simple in design. It concealed few secrets. One end of the upper corridor stopped at a wall, while the other end led to a rotted staircase. A row of dark cells flanked the hall to one side.

The ground floor was more complex. Rather than cells, it held the various rooms of the monastery: a gutted kitchen, a copy room with large drafting tables, a chapel with an altar and pews.

The first floor also led to the solarium, a breezeway that wrapped around the monastery, its awning held aloft by columns. Like the upper corridor, however, anything of value had long since been pilfered.

This was a monastery without crosses or baubles, save for the occasional wooden pendent or rosary bead hidden in a pile of leaves.

Elijah Valero stepped lightly towards the stairwell, but his weight tested the floor. The wood groaned with each footfall. He grimaced. He could not be careless. The floor was so weak that several of the cells had fallen through completely. In the dark, it was possible to step through a doorway and tumble fifteen feet to stone.

Even at its sturdiest, the floor sagged. Valero moved, creating as little noise as possible.

The same could not be said for the Hangman. As Valero approached the stairs, the man's racket issued clearly from below. He kicked through a pile of fallen timbers, cursing and stomping rats as he encountered them. The rodents squealed in horror, adding to the din.

The Hangman chuckled. He was audacious.

The Spider shielded Valero from excitation.

Don't be fooled by his arrogance, she said. *He wants you to drop your guard. He'll invite you to his feast. The Hangman has cunning. He is shrewd.*

Valero moved to the top step and listened. After a tick of silence, he heard the squelch of the man biting into flesh and blood. The Hangman was eating one of the rats, tasting it raw. He spat and choked. Like a cat, he was stripping the skin and fur before partaking.

The wood was so weak it had the pliancy of moss. On the first stair, a shard of wood rolled beneath Valero's step and crumbled. Debris trickled into the cavity below.

The Hangman stopped eating, and all was silent.

Valero had no choice but to move from the weak step, so another batch of splinters fell, soft as rain in the darkness.

"Who's up there?" the Hangman called. His voice was unthreatening, timid. He pretended fright.

Silence fell over the monastery.

Valero went cold. He clutched the revolver and pulled the gun close to his chest. He would kill the man upon sight, he decided. He could not afford to be indecisive. Meekness in the voice would not dissuade him. Although he tried to remain firm, a powerful sense of doubt wedged in his mind. The sincere tone the man achieved bothered Valero.

He damned the feeling, but doubt remained.

Perhaps this was a homeless old scamp, nothing more, in search of food and shelter. The Spider did not compete with this revelation. Her voice was absent. Valero strained to find her. He considered going back to the cell, rifling his satchel and cupping her in his palms. He begged for her surety, her commands, but she had gone.

His doubt grew. Alone, Valero remained frozen on the stairs.

"I ain't meanin' harm," the old man called. "Whatever you are. I had to get off that trail. I got lost. I ain't even got a gun," he said. "Hell, I ain't carryin' nothin'."

A full minute passed. Even the rats shrank away.

"Why don't you come down here?" the scamp called. "Show yourself."

Was the old man afraid of bandits? Or was it ghosts? Valero struggled to think, but his mind was muddy. Quick and multiplying, he couldn't keep his thoughts straight. It was a hundred voices. He wanted to flee back to the cell. Just as strongly, an urge to call out to the old man below seized him. Torn between these ideas, he stood in place.

One lucid idea was persistent. *Lower the hammer on the Colt,* he thought.

When he acquiesced, delicately lowering the hammer into place, another lucid thought followed. *Put away the gun.*

The weapon disappeared into the folds of his overcoat.

Valero tried to calm himself. The heat, the darkness, and the stairwell window full of darting mosquitoes drew him outward, affirming reality. The mustiness returned. Rats resumed their clatter. Valero drew a shaky breath. He experienced a different fear.

You're sick, he thought, and the voice was his. *You're sick like your mother. That's an old man. What harm could he mean you? You were going to kill him.*

I was, Valero thought.

"A traveler," Valero called out. He had to shout. He hadn't, he realized, spoken in several days. His voice sounded odd to him.

The old man walked across the stone floor, trampling debris. He came to the stairwell, and he looked up at Valero's tall shadow. He was a small man, no more robust than a child.

"What you sneakin' about for?" he asked. "Why didn't you make yourself heard? I ain't nobody."

"I thought you were," Valero said.

Be calm, he thought.

He wished he'd remained in the cell. The old man would have left with daylight. Valero descended the stairs, and more splinters, shaken free, tumbled into the cavity below. Valero stopped short of the man. He looked him over. He was gaunt like a starved dog. Scabs on his face and hands gave him the appearance of a leper. He had long grey hair combed with fingers across the top of his bald, sore-covered scalp. Being close to him, Valero experienced a sliver of revulsion.

The old man chuckled. "This your house, friend? Needs some work, but it's almost a goddamned castle. I ain't intrudin', am I?"

"I said I was traveling."

"At least you got your humor. Say, you got anything to eat? You got a little camp goin' up there?"

When the man stepped forward, Valero instinctively stepped back. There was something familiar in the eyes. Fear entered his mind like the bite of lightning.

With that, the Spider returned, subtle and low beneath his thoughts like conscience.

Watch his eyes. He'll lead you to your death. Where's his rope? Where's the noose?

He is the Hangman, Valero thought. *He almost had me. He was coming for me. I allowed him too close.*

"Only extendin' the hand of friendship," the old man said. Unsure, he looked over Valero. "If there's no food up there, you can come hunt rats with me. There's a fire pit in the kitchen down here. Skewer and roast 'em. It ain't a bad way to live."

Valero grew nauseous. He had almost died. Through the coat, he touched the revolver.

Where's his rope? Where's the noose?

The old man cut a path through the rubble, passing through the front alcove where the heavy door, long ago, was stolen for its hardwood. Here nature invaded worst of all. Grass grew through cracks in the floor. Bats inhabited the rafters.

Valero followed, mashing rotten leaves.

"There's a town near?" the old man asked. "That right? Towards the river?"

A town is fit for a hanging, the Spider said.

"Further on," Valero said. "Not far you hit Bone-of-Wellington."

"Pretty name."

He beguiles. Watch him.

The Hangman rattled on. "I found some old rods to make skewers. Down here towards the kitchen."

You're worthless, Elijah. What is it, exactly, for which you wait?

In the darkness, Valero asked, "Why do you travel alone? I've never been tricked by you."

The old man stopped. "The hell?"

"Every time you're alone. I always get you first. She helps me, you know? She's never been on your side. She saw what you did."

The old man furrowed his brow, and it was enough motion to make one of his scabs bleed. "You're like one of those war fuckers, aren't you?"

"She saw you. How many times I gotta tell you that?"

"Hearin' guns in your head. Hell, friend, we'll part ways pronto if you wanna. I'll leave. I'll be goddamned. Like my life ain't a pile of shit as it is. Friend—"

In the darkness, Valero fetched the Colt Navy. He cocked the hammer.

As was customary, the sight of a gun rendered the Hangman a sniveling mess. He begged.

When had he not begged?

——•◆•——

Several miles distant, three men on the bank of a river stopped their conversation and listened to the echo of gunfire. After three shots, quick in succession, the report died. A horned owl called out, perturbed.

"From the hills," Spence remarked. He stood atop the rock. "Odd time of night for that." He chewed the edge of his mustache.

Corbin Blum was unconcerned. He looked at Felix and laughed.

"You'd do all that to your daddy? You're sick in the head, aren't you?"

"No more than the next," Felix said.

Corbin nodded. "Ain't that the truth."

"That was a revolver," Spence said. "I'd say a .36."

He hopped down from the stone. He walked to where water lapped against the shore.

"You may just have it in you," Corbin told Felix. "Time will tell. You've sure as hell thought it through, boy."

CONSTANCE Bray extended her arms and found balance on the beam of the railroad track. It was a humid morning, and dew covered the steel, wetting the fringe of her skirt. She had risen and dressed early. She was alone while the town slept, and it was a good feeling. With grace, she navigated the rail as though it were a tightrope. She walked past the sawmill complex, the flume of which glinted, dipping into a cordoned section of the dark river. The moon was visible in the sky. Men had yet to report to work, so the mill stood tranquilly.

This was her favorite time of morning, quiet and peaceful, with the forest waking. The chatter of birds emanated from the stand of red cedars to her right. The sun remained behind the hills, but a pink hue waited on the horizon. The beauty and stillness wouldn't last, but the fleeting nature made it more valuable. Storm clouds, dark as ash, rolled in from the northwest. It would be a day of storms, of candlelight.

No matter. There was planning to do. She and Hector, who slept soundly—she hoped—had crated most of their belongings. Their home was quite bare, in fact, save for the bed, a few cooking supplies, a handful of books, and suits of clothes. Such was her excitement that she prepared for departure too early. She left herself with nothing but waiting on her hands.

With despair, she looked up the railroad tracks and counted the days until the locomotive would pass through. It would be another week, and every day would be slower than the last.

She walked to the platform that rose behind Rand's Hotel. She stepped onto the planks. Here she and Hector would board the train. Here the crates of belongings and a trunk of clothes would be stacked, waiting. She already smelled the smoke of the engine, puffing clouds as it rolled to a stop, hissing and belching. From here, she and Hector would finally leave Bone-of-Wellington.

Certain she was alone, Constance took a cigarette, half-smoked, from the front of her dress and put it to her lips. It would not do to be seen as a woman smoking in public. There was no dignity in such a thing, but she cared less than she once had. God, how her mother would've berated her for doing what she did. Cigarettes kept a woman slender, didn't they? With a child on the way she needed all the help she could get, she reasoned. Constance lit the cigarette. She took a draw.

It was comical to think the folks *(those dignified citizens)* of the settlement could pass judgment on anybody for anything at any time. They were the sorriest lot of rubbish she ever encountered. What morals could they possess? These people cared little about church. There was no building dedicated to the worship of God. No church, yet there was a vine-covered shack near the river where two whores plied their trade. Such were priorities in Bone-of-Wellington. The graveyard was the closest thing the town had to a church. At least there were crosses. The people cared less for culture. The only music came from a single fiddler named Brigham Conway (who was also the barkeep at Rand's), and they danced to his chicken scratch like buffoons. The only books, save for the meager library she lugged around, came from the residence of Pierce Ryder, a resourceful old man who assumed the roles of doctor, teacher (a role with which she aided), and many other things.

Constance wanted nothing more than to leave Bone-of-Wellington.

She despised it.

She found the name distasteful. She hated to think it, let alone say it.

There was something vulgar about it. According to Pierce, Old Man Argo, the owner of the settlement and the logging camps that fed it, had retained rather than invented the name. Upon coming west, the first Englishman to travel Kinnikinnick River found the skull of a man on this site, he said. This was a century in the past. For some reason, the Englishman named the skull Wellington and buried it in the woods. The river narrowed here, so the man set up a waystation and called it Bone-of-Wellington. He traded with the natives and Spanish missionaries.

Nobody had ever found the buried skull, so Constance guessed the whole thing apocryphal, an invention of the Argo family.

Bone-of-Wellington (or any other designation) was too much name for the place. The haphazard collection of clapboard shanties, pitiful tents wallowing in mud, streets that needed chains to navigate, a stable, Rand's Hotel, and a few offices and stores largely unoccupied deserved to remain nameless. It was a sore on the earth—dirty, stinking, dishonest, oddly slow. Of the fifty odd inhabitants, most were men. There were few children—children being the mark of a growing town, of stability. Bone-of-Wellington would never grow into a city; it was a colony in the forest, one that, when stripped of its treasure (the red cedar), would be left to decompose. Eventually there'd be nothing but a graveyard. Epitaphs would have to tell the story because there wasn't a newspaper to do so.

When the cigarette burned close to her fingers, Constance took a final draw. She flicked what remained over the railing. Turning, the sight of Pierce Ryder approaching with his small, straw-colored dog, Sophia, startled her. At least it was a man she knew and liked. Pierce was one of the few in town who didn't greet her with lecherous looks.

Ryder didn't cut an impressive figure. He was seventy years old, and he'd lived multiple lives in those years. He had the look of a man who had gained and lost a fortune. Hard life left a look of perpetual weariness on his face. To Constance, Pierce struck her as a man stretched thin as gossamer. Regardless, he possessed boundless energy. His eyes were deep and intelligent and somehow youthful. He wore a blue kepi, that of a Union soldier. The hat was crumpled like a smashed paint can. He was never without it.

Sophia rushed up the depot steps and brushed the hem of Constance's skirt. She leapt down to the tracks and combed gravel with her snout. In an instant, she was gone in the woods, yipping, chasing.

Pierce smirked. "Now what would Hector say if he knew you were partaking of a cigarette right out in the open?" He looked up the steps and around at the platform. "On a stage, no less."

"He'd scowl," Constance said. "Then he'd mutter." She thought, then said, "He would be as ornery about it as you are, and he'd be so until I promised not to let it happen again."

"I see." Pierce smiled. "He strikes me as a man who controls his woman."

"Does he now?"

Pierce walked up the steps and joined her on the platform. "Thinking about leaving?" he asked.

"It kept me awake last night," she conceded. "I think of little else."

"Not even that?" He pointed at her stomach.

"It's really the same thing," she said. "I can't think of them separately." She paused and looked across the tracks at Sophia, who appeared beneath the trees. The dog looked manic, somewhat troubled. "Why are you up so early?" she asked.

"I don't know," he said. "A bad feeling, I s'pose. Sophia kept at the door all night. She's still damned nervous. She's frothing a bit."

"I see that."

"Something off."

"Let's hope it's your imagination," Constance said. "I'd hate for Hector to step in any trouble when he only has days left." Communicated lightly, perhaps, but this was one of her chief fears. Hector was not cut out for the work to which he applied himself. In many ways, he was a delicate man. Constance would never say as much, but she felt it. He was not coarse like the others in Bone-of-Wellington.

Pierce walked to the railing.

"God forbid," he agreed.

Something heavy weighed on him. His face was downcast. His energy to banter faltered.

Constance decided to leave him with his thoughts. Like she, he was up early in order to be alone, not to chat.

"Good morning to you, Pierce," she said in parting. "I have to go wake Hector."

"Stop by and see me this afternoon," Pierce said. "You won't believe it, but the Tyler boys' father came to me and wants me to teach them to read again. I can use your help."

"Why would they ever need to read? Is he through saying it's your fault they can't?"

"I should mention he asked me to ask you to teach them to read. That may answer your question."

"Why not ask me?"

"You know Tyler. He's a stick in the mud. He can't talk to a woman sober."

"He's a drunk. I think his boys are, too. I saw them with a bottle in the graveyard once."

"Then I'll tell him yes."

"You can tell him I won't be here come Monday," she said.

With that, she descended the steps.

"Good morning, Connie dear," Pierce called after her.

HECTOR Bray was cleaning his face at the water basin when Constance pulled open the front door. Light fell across the stacked crates and disheveled mattress. A gust of wind rattled and extinguished the candle before him. He pushed aside the razor and small, oval mirror, and he dried his face with yesterday's shirt.

Constance found a stone and propped the door. Strong wind trembled the planks of their home. The door shuddered on recycled hinges. As always, the odor of sawdust fringed the breeze.

"Storm's coming," Constance said.

She was fully dressed. Wind had reddened her pale cheeks. She was, as she had always been to him, surreal in her loveliness. Her black hair was pulled back rather than fixed properly atop her head, but it only accentuated the structure of her face. She had a wide mouth and the slightest hint of an overbite, a feature that turned radiant when she formed a smile.

"My early riser," Hector said.

Constance shouldered past the crates and moved from the antechamber of the cramped shack. Their home consisted of two rooms (which was one more than most of the homes in town): a bedroom and kitchen. Hector brushed his shaving equipment from the dining table as she approached. He opened his arms. She leaned against his bare chest, and he kissed her hair.

"Just restless," she muttered.

"We're almost there," he said.

Constance smiled. She leaned close to his ear and bit playfully at the lobe.

"If only you would've stayed in bed this morning," he said.

She pulled away. "Have you had breakfast?"

He nodded.

"Coffee?"

"Coffee, too."

He pulled a clean shirt from the back of one of the kitchen chairs. Constance had starched the collar. He slid his arms into the shirt and began to button it. He fetched his pocket watch from the table.

"You be careful today," she said. "I saw Pierce this morning and he said he had a bad feeling."

"A bad feeling? Well, he's practically a medicine man, isn't he?" Hector said. "Speaking of, where's that bottle of stomach bitters? I feel sour."

"That's what you get for making your own breakfast." Constance went into the bedroom and returned with the brown glass bottle of Dr. J. Hostetter's. The medicine was a favorite of Ryder's. He prescribed it for anything and everything. It was the one tonic always in stock at the emporium. Hector took a drink and recoiled. The medicine had the impact of smelling salts.

"I mean it," Constance said. "Be careful today."

Hector gave her a long kiss.

"You got it," he said.

———— ·◆· ————

As Hector cut down a side street towards the main thoroughfare of Bone-of-Wellington, the clamor of saws and rolling logs filled the air. Sawdust, thick enough to coat a man's lungs, hung like morning mist, painting shacks as it settled. Wind did nothing to abate the effect.

As Constance said, the sky was darkening. The clouds were thick and grey, piling atop one another. A storm approached. Constance's gloomy portent clung to his thoughts, as though infectious. He, too, had a sick feeling in his gut, a feeling the bitters did nothing to assuage. It was not a feeling with which he wanted to begin his final week as peace officer.

A gust nearly stole the hat from his head, and with the gust came the first drops of rain. Hector quickened his pace. He walked from the alley and took the plank sidewalk, elevated from the muck of the street, towards his office. He nodded at a boy named Wiley, who was leading a horse toward the freshly painted livery stable. The kid returned the gesture.

Hector's place of work was a single-story office with *LAW* branded above the doorway. Abutting the office, a separate shed, with a small window six feet off the ground, was a jail cell labeled *GAOL*. Law was, he'd found in the past year, a complex title. The Argo family, who owned the logging company and sawmill, and who'd only visited Bone-of-Wellington once during Hector's tenure, expected him to not only keep the peace but to serve as a liaison for their lawyers if any other logging company butted in on their business. That situation had yet to arise, but he was told to be prepared if it did. Additionally, and not unlike Pierce Ryder, Argo expected Hector to be something of an intellectual handyman, handling jobs as they arose.

His most immediate duty was to police the sawmill workers, mainly the drunks who gathered at Rand's during lunch and dinner hours. Quite literally, he was expected to keep them from killing one another. His job was to defuse rather than punish. It was not fulfilling work, but the pay was regular. He and Constance managed to save quite a bit over the preceding months, more money than he would have saved back home. It was enough of a nest egg to get started in California. That alone was the reason he took the job.

Across Main Street, chains stretched every twenty feet. Low to the ground, the chains provided traction and kept laden wagons from getting stuck in the morass. Discarded from the sawmill and free for the taking, the chains were a cheaper solution than stone and more permanent than wood. The chains kept traffic moving towards the sawmill and away from it, and they provided the only points to cross the road without sinking into mud and horseshit. They also provided music for the day, being, as they were, outside his office.

Hector crossed delicately at the section of chains closest to his work. He didn't want Constance to feel she needed to wash his boots tonight. In the distance, thunder rolled. The rain stayed light.

A young man waited inside the office, wringing his hands. He was seated on one of the hard wooden chairs, elbows on knees. His face was bloodless, like he was about to black out. When Hector opened the door and stepped inside, he startled the kid. Faint light passed through the window and barely reached the desk and chairs. Most of the office remained in shadow. It was a bare, almost solitary room, a place to sit and talk and sign forms, but not a place where much business was conducted.

The kid shaded his eyes when he looked up at Hector, but that didn't conceal the mixture of confusion and fear on his face. He looked ill. It came to Hector that the kid had witnessed something horrible. His first thought was an accident at the mill. Those machines ate arms and legs.

Hector tried to place the kid's name but couldn't. He wasn't a stranger, though. He'd seen him around.

"Aren't you supposed to be at work?" Hector asked.

He had a pit in his stomach.

Damn it, he thought. *Not today. Not now.*

Hector crossed to the desk, pretended to shuffle the drawers around, and then fetched his brown leather vest from a peg on the wall. He left his gun, unloaded, in the bottom left drawer of the desk. He wore no holster to sheath the weapon. One hadn't been provided, and he wasn't inclined to purchase such a thing.

The kid was in a daze. He was eager to talk but couldn't find a place to start.

"They sent me over here," he said finally. "I've been waitin' on you."

Hector sat on the opposite side of the desk. He faced the young man. He sensed the coffee and eggs on his breath—his mouth was fetid and in need of a rinse.

"What's your name?" he asked.

"Tom Parker. You know me."

"Yeah, I know you. I've seen you anyhow. What'd they send you over for? Don't tell me they're drinkin' already." Hector hoped it was that simple. Constance's portent came to mind. He didn't want to broach the subject. "It isn't fisticuffs, is it?"

The kid shook his head, gathering courage. "It's Felix Hines."

"Okay. Go on."

"He got on at the mill about six months ago. His daddy worked there, too. You know who he is?"

Hector nodded. "Bryson Hines," he said.

Parker halted. Then he said, "The whole family's been killed. Only Felix ain't there. Either whoever did it took him, or he did it."

There it was.

A touch of vertigo passed through Hector. For a second, his head was light and his stomach nauseous. He straightened in his seat, trying to appear composed. A stern countenance was the one defense he had as a peace officer. When one put on the appearance of a stiff upper lip, people believed it authentic. They couldn't see what was in the heart, and they couldn't hear the quickening of a pulse.

Then, after a breath, he doubted Tom Parker. Bone-of-Wellington was a rough-edged hellhole, but it wasn't a place of murder. The only time he'd investigated a killing was when one of the loggers in a camp twenty miles distant killed another man's dog over an argument. That was the closest Hector had come to encountering murder. Parker's face was sincere, though. He wasn't lying.

"Who sent you over here?" Hector asked. "And why you?"

"Jim did, the day foreman. I told him first. He sent me here right then."

"Why you?"

"'Cause I found 'em." Parker's face quivered. His chin twitched. High color replaced the ghostly pale on his cheeks. He used substantial will to hold himself together. He was desperately close to breakdown.

"Doesn't put you in a good spot, does it?"

Gain the upper hand, Hector thought.

"No, sir, it don't, but I'm one of the few people 'round here that liked Felix. I was tryin' to get him in good standing at the mill. That's why I went around this mornin'. He was late all last week. His daddy gave up on him. Felix came in late to piss off Bryson, I suppose. If it weren't for his daddy he'd been fired. I was tryin' to help him."

"You walked in on it?"

"I opened the door, and it was there. It was done already."

Hector knew the name of Felix Hines. He was a quiet kid, a loner who got picked on and didn't do much to defend himself. He was a frail and weak-willed young man. He was not, as far as Hector knew, a troublemaker. His father, Bryson, was a notorious jackass, however. Bryson fit in well with the men in town. Felix did not. The image of Felix working at the mill was almost laughable. It was interesting that he had a protector in Tom Parker. Parker, although young, had a callused look about him, a bull neck and a head like a stone. He fit in fine, despite the bleeding heart.

"Well...." Hector paused.

"Well, what?"

"Well, let's go have a look," Hector said.

It was a hell of a way to begin his final week on the job. Inside he was knotted. The worry that filled his mind was multilayered. If Felix was unhinged, he was a threat to more than his family. Hector thought about Constance, home alone and planning for their first child, for the journey to California, for the rest of their lives. He worried about his ineptitude as a peace officer. He didn't know where to begin when investigating a murder, what to ask, what to look for. First, he guessed, he simply must look at the deed. See it. Maybe something would occur to him. The thought chilled his mettle. After seeing it, he'd dig out the manual Old Man Argo had left in the desk, a handbook of police procedures published in London thirty years prior.

God Almighty, Hector thought.

RAIN turned into a humid mist that clung like wet wool. As Hector followed Tom Parker across the street chains, then down the sidewalk, he steeled himself. Pride kept him from admitting his lack of confidence. Outwardly, the look on his face was one of a seasoned professional. In reality, he'd seen more dead horses than dead men. He didn't know what to expect. He couldn't allow himself to get sick in front of the kid, no matter how grisly. That much he realized.

Between the emporium and a hillside cemetery, a lane of residential shacks jutted out. A few hovels and tents flanked the muddy path. It was squalor, even for Bone-of-Wellington.

Shameful that people live this way, Hector thought. *Shameful you'd bring Connie near this place.*

Another thought, equally shameful, occurred to him. He could take Constance, rent horses from the stable, and leave immediately, shirking the onerous duty placed before him. It would be a small matter to come back and retrieve his belongings later. It would eat into their savings but not greatly. It was a tempting idea, and he almost turned back, but pride spurred him forward.

How right you were about that bad feeling, Ryder.

Lightning cut across the sky. Thunder trembled the ground. The air changed. The trees on the hillside bent with gusts. A sheet of rain, like a grey wall, emerged from behind the hills. The rain moved forward, yard by yard, consuming. Then the mist was banished and a downpour that overturned the mud and made the river leap descended.

Parker led without haste, hands in his pockets, getting drenched.

He's still in a daze, Hector realized. *He could walk directly into the river and not flinch.*

Parker wore no hat. Rain plastered flaxen hair against his scalp and over his ears, turning it dark. He stared ahead and walked on towards the end of the row. Hector crossed his arms atop his head, weighting his hat, and trudged through the mud.

The hovel to which Tom pointed, a single room pieced together with untreated scrap, waited in the shadows. Unlike other homes along the row, there was no lantern light in the crease of the shutters. The shed was eerily still. Rain hammered the roof.

There's no crowd, Hector thought.

Cynically, he expected people to elbow for room, fight for a chance to see the carnage. It was too early by his reckoning, and the weather was too harsh. Most of the settlement was at the mill. The men had gone to work with little thought of the Hines family. The few women and children in town waited beneath leaking roofs, unaware. Aside from Tom Parker and his foreman, Jim Packard, not many people knew.

How will it be when word spreads? he wondered. This was the most peaceful the shack would look for a while.

Parker stopped outside the door. Battered by the rain, he looked at Hector.

"They're still in the bed."

Hector Bray, who was not a veteran of the late war, who was not a man of blood, lowered his arms and stepped to the door. It was a flimsy construct, warped to the extent it would never close. The door reminded him of a gate on a horse stall. He touched the rusted handle and opened the door outward. Without looking, he stepped inside the dark shell, which was full of must and mildew, leaving Parker outside.

To the kid he said, "Go fetch Ryder."

Parker hesitated. Life returned to his eyes.

"Take a look. There ain't nothin' Ryder can do about this."

"Get him anyway," Hector said. In truth, he wanted to be alone. The tang of fresh blood coated his throat. The drum of his heart was in his ears. He didn't want to faint.

Parker said nothing, but he started back in the direction he'd come.

Hector removed his hat and drained the standing water onto the floor. The smell of sleep came to him. The room was hot. The place was a miserable, cluttered hovel. Rivulets of water snaked along the ceiling and dropped into a leather pail in the corner. The clop of the water was rhythmic. As he scanned the room, Hector's mouth went dry. His hands shook. There was light enough to see, despite the storm.

It took him several seconds to take in the scene. He saw only a mass of tangled flesh on the bed. The people didn't seem real. The blood looked like shadow. Bryson Hines, his wife, Cora, and their daughter, Willa, lay together on a narrow straw mattress. There were two straw pads on the floor, additional beds, but both were empty. The three bodies lay together as though carefully arranged. Bryson's arm draped the others, an imitation of sleep. There was something disturbingly domestic about the image—the family sleeping together.

Save for a kitchen table with chairs, the bed was the only piece of furniture in the home. Really, the bed was the centerpiece. Blood, an incredible amount, had soaked into the bed, and now it puddled on the floor below.

Hector gathered his thoughts. He took several breaths. He had to be calm, and he had to think with clarity. When his legs were sure, he looked again.

Footprints pitted the swath of blood on the ground. A single set led from one end of the room to the other, even appearing under the kitchen table. Had the kid taken breakfast after doing the killing?

Felix Hines, as Parker noted, was nowhere to be found.

It didn't take much looking to determine how the family died. Inching closer to the remains of Bryson Hines, whose leg hung off one side of the bed, he realized with a start that the man's head wasn't intact. The same was true for the woman and girl. Hammer blows had shattered their skulls, leaving them grotesquely opened here, caved there. Innards of grey tissue splattered the wall. The weapon, a mallet crusted with hard flesh, lay at the foot of the bed.

God Almighty, Hector thought. He grew lightheaded and ill.

If Felix were responsible, he was a monster. What else could express such rage? And rage it was. A mallet was too personal, too close to the breast for anything less than rage. Unlike with the anonymity of a gun, Felix would have been directly on top of his family as they died. He killed with his hands.

Lightning painted the room white, and then the dreary gloom returned. Despite the rain, Hector walked outside. He'd taken in all he could take. Regardless, a macabre sense of awe overtook him. It was troubling to think all this had gone on under his nose, in his backyard, and neither he nor anyone else had noticed. He and Constance were only a hundred yards distant. The Hines had neighbors on every side.

If there had been screams, no one responded. He wondered if Felix drugged his family. The smashing hammer, the cracking bones went unheard. Felix Hines, if he were responsible, had slipped out the front door while it was dark, and he'd walked past the other shacks. Everyone slept while a murderer walked free.

If he were responsible....

It was a modest attempt to maintain equilibrium, to keep objectivity, but Hector found he'd already made up his mind.

Where is everyone? he thought then, looking about.

The streets remained empty. Hector no longer wanted to be alone. He wanted a mob to share his outrage. Like Tom Parker, he forgot he had a hat to shield against the rain. He walked directly into the leaping mud and shit of the street.

PIERCE Ryder was not formally educated in the doctor's trade. Despite wide learning, he'd never had formal schooling at all. Ever since his mother taught him to read at three years old, though, he educated himself. During the war with Mexico, he went from infantryman to physician's assistant to field surgeon within a matter of eight months. His ascendency was born of talent and necessity. It was on the battlefield that he learned anatomy. He could carve out bullets, saw limbs, and set bones. When that didn't work, he could build a coffin and dig a grave.

Ryder was the closest thing Bone-of-Wellington had to a doctor.

He'd been standing in his work shed, preparing a vat of gruel to cook out back once the rain ended, when young Tom Parker came running through the downpour. At first, he thought the boy a fool, but when he saw the wild look in his eyes, he knew something terrible had happened.

He did not believe too deeply in premonitions, but he kept a dreamcatcher in his home, and he knew a few Indians and Chinese who possessed the ability to foretell events with regularity. On his bookshelf, there was a copy of the *I Ching* beside the *King James Bible*. He was never one with exclusive beliefs.

The night previous, Ryder dreamed Kinnikinnick overflowed and flooded Bone-of-Wellington, washing away everything in a mighty storm. He and Sophia had been nervous ever since. The dog, he believed, often shared his feelings about things. Although he wouldn't freely admit such a thing, Ryder believed it possible his dreams touched her thoughts sometimes.

Tom dashed forward, stopping beneath the awning. Water dripped from his hair, chin, and hands. His chest heaved as he gulped air. He said nothing of floods, though.

"It's Felix," Tom said. "Hector's over there now. It's bad."

"I'll get my bag," Ryder said.

Tom stopped him. He divulged the details as he knew them, speaking in one extended sentence, a breathless rant. When he'd finished it was clear there was no need for gauze and tonic.

Ryder's mind went to Felix Hines. He knew the boy well, more than most. It was not a matter of disbelieving what Tom said, but a matter of not wanting to believe it. In his heart, he knew Felix was capable.

He thought, too, of what Connie Bray said at the depot earlier that morning: *God forbid Hector find trouble now.*

That damn child, Ryder thought.

Felix was an empty husk, capable of no genuine emotion. He was damaged. The boy imitated feelings, but he didn't experience them.

"Hold tight," Ryder said.

Tom stared blankly.

"You can wait here," he added. "Sophia won't go into the rain. You can keep her company."

Tom shook his head.

Ryder stepped to the back of the shed and pulled out a canvas tarpaulin. Generally, he used these to cover graves while in the process of digging them, to protect the holes from filling with rain. In a pinch, they made fine umbrellas. He stretched the tarpaulin over his head and invited Tom to join him. Tom did so, extending the canvas over his head.

"At Bryson's," Tom said.

With that, they dashed into the rain. Sophia stood beneath a sawhorse. Wary and unwilling to get wet, the dog remained behind.

Outside the shack, Hector stood in the rain. Ryder and Tom hurried forward, splashing through the street while rain drummed their makeshift umbrella.

"Is it bad?" Ryder asked, shouting over the wind.

Hector gestured at the shack.

Ryder left Tom with the canvas and stepped through the open doorway. The mud on his boots squelched against the floor. The old man didn't advance deeply into the room. He stopped and stood rigid, like an open hand had fallen against his face. The tension was infectious. The cruelty was enough to make a man weep. A buzzing fly (*they were always so quick to descend,* he thought) crawled in the shards of Willa Hines' skull, lifting and landing, lifting and landing. Hard blood crusted the young girl's dark hair. Ryder was light in the head.

"By God, I delivered her," he muttered, remembering the moment as if it were a defense against the image. The memory only made what he saw more grievous.

From his coat, Ryder withdrew a flask. He took two long drinks and then handed the liquor to Hector, whose frame filled the entryway. The peace officer took a sip. When he found it was brandy and not rotgut, he drank a mouthful. Life returned to his eyes.

"Son, you're gonna have to act on this," Ryder said. "There isn't time to tarry. They're already gonna wonder why you haven't called a posse together. Each minute's going to weigh on you."

"You ever see anything like this?" Hector asked. "Pierce, I don't—"

"—Go get your gun," Ryder said.

He had to be firm and resolute. Softness would only hurt both men. Hector had a glazed look.

"Tom and I will meet you up at the mill. Hey, now. You hear me? Hector, you gotta get your sand together. Like it or not, you got a job to do."

Even as he spoke, he thought, *Poor Connie. What'll she do now?*

"I haven't ever—"

"There isn't anything to know, son. You gotta run him down. He's a kid and green, but he's got several hours on you. Get your gun. Get a horse outta the stable. Pick some men. Head out."

"You think it was Felix?"

Ryder hesitated. He swallowed a lump in his throat.

"Ashamed to say so, but I'd almost guarantee he did this. How well did you know Felix?"

"I didn't know him at all," Hector admitted.

"I did. I let him borrow a few books. I talked to him quite a bit. One time I caught him with a stray cat. He kicked the thing so hard he caved in its ribs. I never told him I saw him. After he did it, he stood there and looked at the cat. It was writhing. To me, he reacted to it the same way he read books. Nothing ever hit him. It was all intellectual. Just things happening. He *could* do something like this, and that's not something I'd say about many."

Hector stared, not listening, lost in thought.

Ryder pushed him out the door. "You gotta get to the mill," he said.

FELIX tugged to make the horse follow. Although the mare didn't mind rain, the thunder made her skittish. Felix made her skittish, too. Maureen had never liked him. When she planted her hoofs, he dragged, cursed, and switched her snout.

Maureen watched him with utter hatred. She would kill him given the chance. She was not alone. After this morning, there were many who fit into that category.

I struck first, Felix thought with pride. *They can't hurt me when I strike first.*

As he and the mare neared the top of the hill, Felix stopped in a pine grove.

Ahead, through the dark veil of the storm, stood an open gateway where a massive wooden door once towered. Felix forgot the mare, and he looked upward. The monastery, the same he had been told about since childhood, came into view. The ornate fence of the courtyard garden had been chipped like so much chalk. The wall looked like a victim of war, cratered by gunshot. Rain left the stone a dark beige. Vines grew over the wall. The wall was stone in the front section, but it had been wood elsewhere. The fence no longer stretched around the monastery—at the sides, the fencing had long since rotted into the earth.

Beyond the wall and across a garden courtyard stood the monastery proper.

Heightened by the storm, with rain whipping its exterior, the ruins held a gothic quality. A belfry with gaping holes loomed over the forest like a watchtower. The protrusion leaned, threatening to topple with the next strong gust.

The sight was everything Felix imagined it to be.

Steeped in decay, rot clung to the monastery's bones. Moss and vine laced the façade in systems intricate as roots. Time had ravaged the exterior. Windows opened like hollow eye sockets over the garden. The tiled roof was caved in sections, exposing dark holes, while it supported crumbling chimneys in others.

The structure impressed, rising as it did two stories from the forest, crowning the hill. The encroaching woods infused the place with a hidden, cryptic feel.

The arcading that formed a walkway around the base was particularly beautiful. Felix had never seen stone arches, and here arches followed one another in a procession around the contour. The permanence of a stone building was at odds with everything he knew in Bone-of-Wellington. It was easy to believe that Spanish monks came here to hide from the world and seek converts among the Indians. This fortress had all that history woven in its fibers.

Despite the ignorance of his father and mother, Felix was well read. Unlike them, he appreciated beauty, even the beauty of decay. He knew the world intellectually, if not through experience. He'd seen illustrations of stone castles, abbeys, and cathedrals. The library of Pierce Ryder had been his teacher. Ryder was the only man to own books of merit in the settlement, so Felix gravitated to him. Felix read *The Iliad* and *The Odyssey,* and he read novels by the likes of Matthew Lewis and Anne Radcliffe—thick, absorbing tomes. The monastery looked like it had come from one of those dark English stories.

It was from another world.

Felix hastened forward, pulling at the mare until she acquiesced. She was angry enough to kick out his guts, so he stayed clear of her reach. He hated the horse as much as she hated him. He yanked the reins until leather bit into her flesh. When she hurt, she moved. He spat at her front hoof.

Felix wanted to remember this moment. It was one of the finest moments of his life. He wouldn't allow the horse to ruin it.

After listening for approaching riders, which were absent from the forest, he walked through the front gate.

NINE

ELIJAH Valero awoke on a pew, feeling dazed, almost drunk. He'd had no liquor, he was acutely aware, for over a month. Perhaps he'd dreamed of whiskey and gin, because sobriety was unwelcome. Behind his eyes, his head throbbed. Delicately, he swung his feet around and planted them on the cool floor. The craving for a drink grew.

A chest full of smoke wouldn't be bad, either, he thought.

With some fortune, he'd buy a woman, too. The self-imposed asceticism caught up with him all at once, and he was irritable and grumpy.

Valero decided to leave the monastery.

He did not feel paranoid. There were no voices in his mind, save for his. The thoughts, as they'd been for the past two days, were his. Although he would not tempt her presence by denying her, he was certain the Spider had retreated to the hole from whence she came. Such was her way. She had come and gone ever since Valero was a young man. Now, in his thirties, the stints when she was present became longer and longer, often lasting months. This time the Spider pestered him with demands for nearly four months.

When she was gone, she was gone. Sometimes she stayed away for weeks, sometimes half a year.

Although irritable, he also felt peaceful, listening to rain on the wooden rooftop. The roof leaked heavily, droplets falling twenty feet to the floor, but his pew remained dry through the night.

Valero hoisted his satchel from the ground, rummaged its contents, and then he pulled out a stub of tack bread. It was hard enough to chip teeth, but at least it wasn't wormy. With effort, he cracked off a piece, then dropped the remainder of the biscuit in his bag. He was in sore need of real food. Shamefully, Valero ate more than a few rats, bony themselves, over the past few weeks. He ate a bird that fell dead in the belfry. He managed to shoot a few rabbits and a coyote. That was the extent of meat in his diet.

While walking in the forest a few days prior, he caught sight of his reflection in a puddle. His face was gaunter than he'd ever seen. The markings of a skull emerged beneath his skin. His features were sunken, his dark beard long and unruly, his eyes like black knots. He saw the thinness in his arms and legs, too. He'd lost thirty pounds over the last few months. He looked ill, near death. Seeing his face in the puddle had made him recoil. A stranger stood in place of the man he knew.

What have you become? he had thought.

It would take a month of carnal pleasures to fatten him up, but for that he needed money. He'd exhausted every penny that came from selling his grey mare. The money dried up quickly. The horse was gone, and the money was gone. The thought of leaving his horse behind shook his heart. He hoped the girl was doing all right, that she was pleased. He sold the mare in too much haste to check up on the fellow who purchased her.

She could be dog meat, he needled.

He sold a friend, and that type of shame didn't pass. Morose, he stood from the bench.

The chapel spread around him, a husk like the rest of the monastery. The wooden altar remained, and the benches were left behind. The high ceiling, which stretched to the height of the first and second floors, was the only majesty left in the chapel. There were no statues of Jesus, no Virgin Mary. Monks, or those who followed the monks, had carved words into the benches, sometimes names, sometimes epistles, but it was all in Spanish or Latin. To Valero, their words were as indecipherable as hieroglyphs. He could only admire the practiced elegance of the handwriting. He liked the chapel because, unlike the cells upstairs, it stayed cool. The windows were open to the wind and rain. The air moved here better than any other room. The cells were designed to be uncomfortable and stifling. There was also the matter of the old man above. Valero hadn't checked on the man in days. He wanted to avoid the memory.

An unfamiliar voice from the outer hall brought Valero to full attention. He tensed, listening. Quietly, he put on his long coat. He tucked his greasy hair beneath a worn black hat. After pulling the Colt from his satchel, he draped the leather bag over his shoulder. He held the gun a moment, listening more closely, before slipping the weapon into the inner pocket of his coat.

Indeed, the monastery had a visitor.

"Don't you run off," the man outside *(or was it a boy?)* said. "Goddamn you."

The kid rattled on, berating a horse. He talked fast. He was too self-absorbed and clumsy to have anything to do with Valero. Still, his presence was unwelcome.

Valero slipped from the benches into the center aisle. Again, he stood and listened. The chapel was light enough to see from end to end, although shadows filled the corners. A few drops of rain splashed the side of his boot.

He pulled the Colt again. He stopped short of cocking the hammer.

A boy, with the height of a man but the shoulders of a child, passed the entrance. He wore no hat, nor did he carry gear. His hair was a tangle of brown curls. He gesticulated frantically, oddly, mumbling to himself. He didn't see Valero's shadow in the center of the room. He hadn't bothered to look. His footfalls against the stone grew fainter.

It's only a kid, Valero thought, shaking his head. *Probably from the town.*

He put away the gun. Straightening the satchel, he then started towards the chapel entrance, an arched doorway. He waited until the kid headed up the stairwell before he passed into the hallway. With haste, Valero moved towards the arcaded solarium where weeds sprouted. He'd walked here for fresh air many times, but the monastery was no longer a comfort to him. He was eager to be gone from this place, its rot and its whispers. It reminded him of things he had no desire to remember. With a clear mind, he had no more need for the isolation it offered. Outside, the storm had largely abated. The wind calmed. The rain lightened to mist. The sun gilded the edge of a cloud.

The kid had tied his horse to one of the columns. Valero watched her strain to lap up a puddle on the ground. She couldn't quite reach it, and she was miserable. The sight was pathetic. She was once a pretty gal, a chestnut brown roan with white socks, black mane. Hard work ravaged her youth. Hard life destroyed her elegance. Idleness in old age robbed the last of her vigor.

Valero walked up to the mare and petted her face. She had a good heart. He saw it in her eyes. That made him all the angrier when he noticed the bloody stripes that scarred her flank. She had cuts on her snout, too, where the boy struck her face. It looked like the kid beat her for the hell of it. A film of sweat covered her body. The saddle hung loose on her back, and the straps had chafed her belly. Valero loosened her reins from the column. She dipped her head and went to the water.

"Looks like we need each other," Valero whispered. "How 'bout it?"

When the puddle was gone, the mare raised her head. She didn't protest as Valero adjusted her saddle. She had no qualms about thievery, nor did he. Looking back inside the monastery, Valero saw no sign of the kid. He heard footsteps on the old planks of the second story.

Happy exploring, Valero thought. He tipped his hat.

He mounted the horse, and then he eased her through the arches and the briar patch garden. The rain was finished, replaced by a hot, humid morning. The mare, Valero thought, was pleased. Horses know. Her tail snapped in defense of the awakening insects, and there was some vigor in the snap.

Sometimes life falls into place, Valero thought.

EXPOSED to the damp forest by an arched window, the stairs had succumbed to nature. The steps flaked and bowed beneath Felix's boots. Ascending into the shadowed hall brought a thrill. He had never asked for extravagant things, and he wondered why his father had denied him this pleasure.

There were a couple other boys, Tom Parker and Bennie Wolf, who'd seen the monastery on hunting trips. This place was old news to them. Bennie, who was a bully and braggart, mocked Felix for his puritanical father. When they were thirteen, Bennie crushed Felix's lip, the hardest he was ever hit, over some remark Felix didn't recall. Tom stood up for him then, wrestling Bennie to the ground. It was the moment he and Tom became friends.

When the opportunity came, Felix mused, he'd take the hammer to Bennie Wolf, too. He often fantasized about ripping Wolf with saw teeth. He was curious to see how human skin would appear when curled on the teeth of the blade. It would look like cheese, he assumed, curled in tiny petals.

In the upper corridor, Felix discovered a wide walkway, fallen through in places, bustling with rats. The amount of vermin was incredible. A mix of leaves, rodent carcasses, feathers, bird droppings, pieces of the ceiling, and insect husks blanketed the floor. Each step was a crunch. Some of the rats were dead, their bellies bloated, feet turned to the ceiling. Other rodents, unconcerned, scurried about their business. Felix's presence made no difference. The rats had safety in numbers.

A row of open doorways, monk cells, dominated one side of the hall. The frames were narrow, intentionally small. The other side of the corridor was a blank wall, chipped and eaten through in swaths, pierced with empty nails where crosses had been. Coiled bats rested in the holes.

Felix weaved through the labyrinth of scuttling bodies towards the cells. In one of Ryder's books, he learned that monks followed something called the contemplative life—a life devoted to meditating about things. To Felix, the idea was fantastic. Every season, one of books and quiet. How fortunate those men were. He could endure that type of solitude. He would have been a monk if born in the right place and time. He even liked to think about God, which was something of a prerequisite, he imagined, but he preferred Homer to King James.

At that, he had to smile. The atmosphere of the place forced him to lose sight of himself. With the beliefs he chased, the monks would've cast him out. This was a house for the God of the Living. The monastery fit him better in its abandoned state.

Felix peered into the cells. Some were in fair condition. The floors were sturdy, the walls solid, the ceiling closed. Other cells had decayed beyond repair. In a couple cells the floor had fallen through completely. Here the doorways opened upon jagged holes. Felix investigated one of the holes and spotted a dark pile of rubble below, teeming with more rats. With his imagination running wild, he looked for a face in the rubble, a hint of thorns. He wondered if Bone-of-Wellington were abandoned, how long it would take for rats from the river to descend and take over the mill and the homes surrounding it.

A *matter of days.*

As Felix approached the final cell, the buzz of flies became apparent. The thrum was jarring in the empty hall, so loud that he wondered if the cell held a colony of bees. Oddly, the rats were most abundant in this corner, entering the cell in such a stream it appeared like a choreographed procession. For every rat that entered, one exited.

Drawing still closer, the stench of rotten meat jolted Felix. His pulse quickened. His thoughts numbed to silence. He had only the urge to look, to see. He was both drawn and repulsed. He covered his mouth and nose. Nausea spread through his body and brought a cold sweat to his face. It was primitive revulsion, pure. Felix wondered if someone had stuffed the remains of a deer carcass in the cell. A hunter, perhaps. He'd smelled the rotten offal of deer. This odor possessed a grittier edge.

Felix stepped in front of the doorway. His palms sweated.

Propped in the corner, with its back against the wall, its half-eaten legs pointing toward the center of the room, was a human cadaver.

Felix gasped and panted. His chest heaved.

Where it survived, the corpse's skin had a waxy, wet quality. A tracing of the finger left indentations. Rats covered the body like so much refuse, biting eagerly. Thousands of flies explored the meat and cavities, walked the bones. Where a pocket of gas had torn open skin around the navel, maggots writhed. Roaches scurried beneath the flank and around the heels of the feet. The corpse had become a habitat. It was an odd demonstration of greed.

Felix experienced greed, too. He had never seen something so fascinating. With effort, he calmed his breathing. He uncovered his mouth and nose.

It was a human, and that was all Felix determined. The figure was slight, but he couldn't tell whether it was man or woman, young or old. There were clues. The rags it wore suggested a man, and a vagabond at that. A couple gunshots had blown away half the skull, leaving the bottom jaw intact and little else. He couldn't see where the rest of the head had gone. The man was shot in another location. Someone moved him here, as if this were his tomb.

A rat burrowed into the man's exposed gullet, the rodent's back end where the man's tongue had been. The fleshy tail flicked back and forth like a whip atop the neck, twitching with delight at the feast.

Another thought, more mundane, struck Felix.

Whoever did this could still be here.

He turned and ran, stomping rats as he went. The insect husks made the noise of crushed gravel. He descended the stairs with a few leaps. Stopping below, his chest heaving painfully, he vomited on the floor. The stench had imprinted in his nostrils. Even at this distance, the stench was all around him, foulness in his clothes and hair like smoke. He groped for the revolver at his waist.

Felix tried to calm himself then.

It could be Corbin. He could've done this.

"Corbin! Spence!"

He didn't like the sound of his voice against the stone. It chilled him.

If not Corbin, if not Spence, then whom?

Terror struck Felix. He was caged. Without another thought, he sprinted towards the solarium where he'd left Maureen. He would ride hard and fast until the rot was cleansed from his lungs. It wouldn't be so easy to rid his mind of the image of the feeding rats, the kings of the colony bloated, fat, and engorged.

The horse was gone.

Again, Felix panted. The world seemed to move even as he stood firm.

He wondered if he tied her someplace else. He looked up and down the solarium. He looked into the garden. He hadn't. She was gone.

He's taunting me, Felix thought. *Whoever did this, he's taunting me.*

Cursing, he stumbled into the garden, aiming the revolver in every direction.

"Come out!" he shouted. "I'm here! You have me! Come out!"

You don't know what I've done, Felix thought. *You don't know what I'm capable of doing.*

His taunt remained internal. He wished Corbin were here to have his back. Felix was tired of being alone.

You killed your father. You killed your mother. You killed your sister. She was young, too. She didn't fight. She didn't even fight when she saw what you had done. She only looked at you. She trusted you.

You've done terrible things.

The monastery was silent, save for its wildlife. Uncertain, Felix escaped into the woods. He turned the fear over and over again, until the emotion became tinged with exhilaration.

BEING AN ACCOUNT OF THREE COFFINS
AND THREE GRAVES ON THE EDGE
OF THE KINNIKINNICK RIVER.

RISING commotion shattered her chance of reading. Constance put aside the novel, a piece of Horatio Alger claptrap, and moved to the open doorway. People gathered in the street. Nervously, Constance stepped outside. She approached a family that lived across the way, amassed on their front porch. The husband, Jim Packard, was at work, but his wife and two boys huddled and talked.

Emily Packard turned, watching Constance. She didn't smile, nor affect any greeting.

"Did you hear?" she asked.

Constance shook her head.

Before Emily went on, one of her boys interjected. "Felix done his family in," he said.

"He what?"

"Even his sister," the other boy added. "Men are over there right now. They're gatherin' up a posse."

Behind the boys, Emily nodded. She was not one to be silent, but she was shocked, holding tightly to her sons.

Dear God, Constance thought.

Without another word, she turned and made haste towards Main Street.

Had Ryder known? It was an ignorant thought, and she pushed it away. The old man wouldn't have left her in suspense.

Drawn shutters and watchful eyes filled the windows of the shacks she passed. The whole town teetered on a razor edge, poised with tension. When Constance entered Hector's office, she found her husband, his nose in a manual, behind his desk. Her fear turned to anger. She was wounded.

"When were you going to tell me?" she asked.

Hector looked up as if he expected to see her at this moment.

Seeing the look on his face, Constance cried.

"It's snowballing on me," he said. "I didn't know what to do. There'll be men from the mill here soon." He paused. "I hoped Ryder would come tell you."

"It's true then."

Hector nodded. "Bryson, Cora, and Willa."

"Resign," she demanded.

"Connie—"

"—There's any number of men who will step in and take your place. You're practically finished here. Don't make it your concern. Hector, please."

Hector looked at the ground. The office was silent. He placed the manual on the desk.

"That's a damned callous thing to say."

Constance was still. She considered turning and leaving. She considered smacking his face. In the end, she only wiped tears from her eyes. There was a touch of guilt in her manner, but she felt no heartache for the dead. She begrudged them for drawing Hector into their orbit.

"He killed three people," Hector said.

She drew a shaky breath.

"Then he's a monster. It doesn't matter what happens to him."

"I can't argue with that."

"They'll lynch him," she said. "Let them."

"I probably will."

"And you have to be there for that? You can't just turn the other cheek?"

Hector stood. He walked to Constance. In the shaft of sunlight at the doorway, he wrapped his arms around her and buried his face on her shoulder.

"I feel like I do," he admitted.

"I want you to resign. These people aren't our concern. They never were."

Hector raised his head. He moved back to his desk and lifted the manual.

"I only need to read this," he said. "Everything I need to know is here."

"You're ignoring me."

"I know what you want, and I'm saying no."

"That's all there is to it?"

"I can't leave," he said.

With that, Constance turned and left. She stopped on the porch and sobbed so heavily that passersby mistook her flood of emotion for grief over the Hines family.

AT the base of the hill atop which the monastery stood, the road widened to a thoroughfare large enough to support a Concord coach. By no means was the road in good condition for traveling. Persistent seasons of rain carved labyrinthine ruts in the earth. In places, the ground was treacherous. Horses moved with their eyes here, navigating so slowly it was quicker to walk with the horse rather than ride in the saddle.

Elijah Valero walked beside the roan mare. He had yet to win the girl's trust because she remained jittery. He wondered if her eyesight was faltering, and if she believed him to be the boy they left behind. Valero talked to her as they walked along, venting his mind. Occasionally, she snorted and shook her head. Flies out of the wood line harassed her thighs, and of those she was more concerned. Valero lifted his hat and swatted at the flies.

I'll win you over yet, he thought.

She switched her tail.

When the stone outcropping of a hillside jutted into the path, the road bent sharply. The shade was deeper here, the sun breaking apart in the treetops. The trees were so tall and thick the forest appeared virgin. It was no wonder the forest was earmarked for logging. Every red cedar along the route was a fount of wealth. To whom that wealth belonged, Valero did not know, but someone owned it.

The road opened into a straight stretch on the other side of the bend. A small pond, a pool at the base of another hillside, abutted the path. Valero decided he and the horse could use a plentiful helping of the water. It looked clean. A trickle between the rocks fed the pool. As Valero approached, he released the horse's reins. The pond drew her like a magnet. She walked ahead, bounding over a ditch into a stand of weeds.

There were other men at the pond. Two men, one tall, one much shorter and stouter, were deep in council. They had a wagon, led by two dark horses, and another saddled steed off to the side of the road. As if it were night, and the pond a campfire, Valero announced himself as he stepped from the rutted pathway and into bramble. It was an unnecessary gesture, but one of wariness.

The men were not worried or surprised, but they halted the words they shared. The men had flat, expressionless looks. The tall one had one living eye and one dead eye. The other wore a mustache that would have suited a fashionable man back east. The tall one raised his hand as a greeting.

Valero mistrusted him immediately. Regardless, he reciprocated the gesture. Valero said nothing further. Burdened with heavy thirst, he knelt at the muddy edge of the pond, and he lowered cupped hands into the water. He drank deeply, palmful after palmful. When he felt like he'd slosh, he used the water to clean his face and beard and the back of his hot neck.

The tall man approached, while the stout one remained on the other side of the water.

"How goes it?" the man asked.

"Fair," Valero said.

"You know, I knew a man said he owned the only body of water in a hundred miles. He tried to charge for a drink. He guarded it with a fuckin' shotgun."

The man gave Valero a bad feeling. There was something in his bearing. Even now, he stood too close as he spoke. He laughed a hollow laugh.

"I got no money," Valero said.

"Didn't mean it like that, pal. Just joshin'."

Valero stood. The man was taller than he thought. He had several inches on him, and Valero stood a full six feet.

"Not lookin' for any trouble," Valero said.

The tall man looked him over.

"By god, you're a sad fuckin' sight. You in trouble?"

"Nothin' of the kind," Valero said. He glanced at the mare, who, unfazed, drank.

"Somethin' 'bout you, like maybe I seen you around. Who are you?"

"Just a graveyard ghost," Valero said.

The tall man's dead eye socket quivered.

"Lookin' at you, I'd be inclined to believe it. Goin' our way?"

He pointed towards the monastery.

"The opposite," Valero said.

"Bone-of-Wellington. That's a real shithole. I hear there's trouble brewin' there, too."

"Not my concern."

"That's good to hear. Maybe a graveyard ghost will fit in just perfect with those folks."

Valero looked across the pond. The other man had gone. Valero nodded to the tall man, then he fetched his horse. He'd have to use his gun if he stayed longer.

"Shit, I recognize that fuckin' horse, too," the man said as Valero regained the stage road.

The tall man's compatriot stood at his side. He nodded assent.

"Graveyard ghost," the tall man muttered, and he laughed.

The other man remained somber, his back to the glistening water, staring at Valero until he was out of sight.

HECTOR made the ordeal legal by reading a line from the manual. The Argo family had left the book of procedures in his office, and he was assured the text was all the training he'd need. He'd opened it five times during his tenure, four this morning. Hector shut the book and looked over the men, the peace officer with his crew of deeply angry sawmill workers.

"You're all deputies now," he said.

A lynch mob and perfectly legal.

The thought didn't arrive without guilt. Hector was torn between what he wanted to do and what he should do.

Pierce Ryder stood among the workers, although he'd declined to be deputized. He cautioned the men to stay their hands, to fight the urge for retaliation when they found young Felix. Ryder knew the boy, he said, and there was something wrong with him. He wasn't right in the head. The law would handle things, he promised, eyeing Hector, if allowed to run its course.

Hector groaned aloud. He felt anything but dutiful. He wanted to be with Constance on a train heading south to Trinity Hill.

Although ashamed of the fact, he hoped the men would rend Felix, hang him from a tree, and save everyone trouble. It was not his desire to track the boy, regardless of how heinous his crime, through a hundred miles of forest.

The men dismissed Ryder.

Frank Wolf said, "Don't worry, Gravedigger, you'll get your fee when we finish with him."

Frank's son, Bennie, was among the deputies. The two men were enjoying the way the day unfolded. They had the look of men on a hunt. They insisted, despite Hector's misgivings, upon being involved.

"Better have a grave ready," another man said.

"Go ply your trade," said yet another. Extending his hand from his chest, he said, "He's about yea high, if I recall. About yea wide."

Disgusted, Ryder left the office without another word. Gone was the voice of reason. The door slammed behind him. The old man had no energy to fight the men or aid Hector. Judging by the look he gave before departing, though, it was clear he hoped the peace officer would be the source of authority in his stead.

You're it, he seemed to say. *I'm too old to fight this fight. You're going learn something about yourself today.*

Hector nearly went after Ryder to plead his case. The man had to see the futility of it. Placing Hector in this position was unjust.

Who cared about the boy's rights?

The kid's a killer, a murderer, Hector thought. *There was a young girl in that room. He killed his mother. Is there a worse crime, a more damning indictment of a man? To kill your mother? He even killed her up close, face-to-face.*

Matricide, the manual called it.

Felix Hines left Bone-of-Wellington wearing his family's blood. What place did reason, law, sanity, or decency have in his capture and treatment? He dissolved any rights he'd possessed. Even if captured, he would be convicted and hanged. The end would be the same.

Why be deliberate about the means?

Oil and water, though, were his feelings. The protest, no matter how often Hector mounted it, did nothing to mask the sense of responsibility he had. When it came time, he'd consider Ryder's position, and the old man knew it. Pretending he was enthusiastic kept up his courage.

Hector called Tom Parker from the group.

"Tom, you knew Felix well. I want you to lead one wing of the search. I'll take the other. You up to it?"

"He's up to it."

It was Alf Parker, Tom's grandfather, the man who raised him. He was a rough weasel of a man, cruel and hard.

Tom nodded assent. His demeanor hadn't improved since the morning. He was shattered. Yet, he had qualities men like Alf Parker and Frank Wolf only pretended to possess. He had a decent heart, and he had a temper capable of mercy. Without Ryder, Hector would have to rely on him.

"My guess is he took the stage road," Hector said, addressing the group. "Ain't many other options if he wanted to avoid the lumber camps. I'll take the east, and, Tom, you head west."

"I got a feeling," Tom said softly. He looked at Alf for approval, which he received in the form of a curt nod, then went on. "He always talked about the old monastery. When he was little, he always got mad about how Bryson wouldn't take him there. He asked me about what it was like a few times."

"That's a good place to meet up. We'll converge there," Hector said.

After dividing the mob, Hector sent Tom on his way. Along with five men, including his grandfather, Tom left the office. He wasn't eager for command. If Tom were inclined to allow it, then Alf would take over once Bone-of-Wellington was out of sight. Maybe the boy would surprise him.

Hector left six men for his group, including the Wolf family (he wasn't so cruel as to give that burden to Tom). He led the deputies onto the street, where, shifting in the mud, stood a batch of tethered horses. Wiley, the kid who worked the livery, was adjusting the saddles. He was reluctant to let the horses go.

Tom's group had already mounted, and they were heading through the street. The cross chains jingled as the horses passed over. Without expression, Tom glanced at Hector before turning the corner.

Hector nodded.

Free of the mud, the men spurred their horses and were gone.

"Peace Officer, you inclined to move your ass yet?"

Frank Wolf, high atop his agitated horse, looked down at Hector. He sneered, and then he spat into the mud. "My boy can run a better outfit than you. Almost like you want Hines to get free."

"Then he'd just have to bury the bodies," another man agreed.

"You should go wait this thing out with Ryder," Frank said. "Then you fellas can blather about it all you desire."

Hector mounted his horse. He stretched his back in the saddle and took the point position. He didn't allow the men to bait him.

"I'm here, ain't I?" he said. "Let's head out."

Across the street, shaded by a canopy, stood Ryder, watching. Constance was beside him, demure and slender, dressed for more rain that wasn't coming. Seeing her there, the look on her face, shook his heart.

Hector turned from Ryder and Constance, spurring his horse towards the stage road.

Who is it that you want to protect? He aimed the question at himself, not the old man.

When Frank Wolf challenged his point position, riding up to his side, Hector said, "If we find him, you know what to do."

"Atta boy," Frank said.

Soon the riders were a full mile into the muggy forest.

HE was several miles into the woods when he came upon the posse of riders. They were rough men, armed and hostile. There was only one ineffectual rider among them, and he, to Valero's surprise, rode at the head of the guard. He wore a badge on his clean leather vest, and he was the only one with a badge.

Valero mapped the quickest route to his Colt. Being one man in the face of seven, however, he kept his hands on the reins of the mare. He slowed as the posse approached. His horse was in no shape to outrun them. She'd fall dead in the road. He moved to the side of the path, hoping they'd pass.

Even if only for a second, Valero listened for the Spider. She bade no warning, offered no command. With all the things he'd done, it was always a possibility that men like this were searching for him. He'd be a convenient target. Most of the crew looked like hangmen.

The lead rider raised his hand to halt Valero. He was young, clean-shaven, and had an unsoiled appearance the others didn't possess. He looked sorely out of place. His clothes were pristine, as if a wife tended him.

"That's Bryson's horse alright," one of the men said.

The man with a badge nodded. He shared the look of recognition.

"Stranger," he hailed, "where'd you find that horse?"

He gripped a Smith and Wesson in one hand. Two of the men in the posse cradled rifles. One of the riflemen stopped his horse and jumped to the ground. He hit the dirt with a thud. Slowly but deliberately, he had the rifle against his shoulder and aimed. He came around the side, approaching Valero.

"I found it wandering," Valero said. "I needed a mount."

The man with a rifle sneered.

"Maybe it weren't Felix that did it," he said. He had a red face and curly hair, and he was a bull.

In his condition, Valero was in no shape to tussle with the man, but he figured a bullet would halt him as quickly as any other. He caught the man's eye to warn that, if it came to shooting, he'd die first.

The young sheriff tried to defuse the rising tension.

"There's no need for a story," he said. "We're after one person, and one only. It ain't you. Now, in truth, you didn't find that horse, did you? Where'd you get it?"

"Call off your bull," Valero said.

"Frank, damn it, take a step back, and put your gun down."

Frank spat. He had a mouthful of tobacco.

"Mangy dog," he mumbled.

"What's that?" Valero asked.

"I said you're a starved dog, boy. You ain't nothin' to worry about anyway. Maybe I just feel like bustin' you up."

Valero nodded. The urge to kill the man flashed hard in his mind but doing it here would be ignorance. He was not so youthful as that. He noted the face. He wouldn't forget it.

"The horse?" the sheriff asked. He put away his gun. He leaned on the saddle horn. "Where?"

"There's a monastery not far from here. A couple hours." Valero shifted on the horse. "She looked beaten. Some kid had her tied up. I took her."

"Thief, too," Frank said.

Valero turned. "Aim your gun again," he said. "See what happens."

Frank scoffed, but he didn't aim the weapon.

"You see the kid?" the sheriff asked.

"Briefly. Not well."

"But he was there?"

Valero nodded.

"What's your name, stranger?"

"Eli Valero."

A brief silence passed through the riders.

"Oh hell, I heard of you," another of the men said. He was stout, younger than the rest, bringing up the rear of the posse. "Ain't no way this mutt is Eli Valero." He laughed.

Yet another said, "If he ain't lyin', Frank, you better watch your ass. A real killer he is. A gunman."

Frank joined the laughter.

"Ain't no way," Frank agreed.

The sheriff also recognized the name, although he was not laughing.

"Valero's a gunman," he said. "You sure you didn't steal that name along with the horse?"

A mix of rage and shame came to Valero.

"Did you kill the boy?" the sheriff asked. His tone was hopeful.

"I didn't."

"Hell," Frank said, turning away. "Let's get up to the ruins. If Felix is on foot, he won't get far."

"What'd the kid do?" Valero asked.

"Well, to put it lightly, he killed three members of his family," the sheriff said. He tipped his cap, straightened, and then edged his horse around Valero. "And, hey now,

Mr. Valero, do me a favor. Drop that horse at Bone-of-Wellington, would you? Don't make us come after you, too."

Valero eyed Frank as he passed.

"How 'bout I wait for you?" Valero said. "I'd hate to have to put you through any trouble."

The horses beat the mud, and then they were off.

Valero dismounted and walked to the front of the mare. She was trembling, no longer fighting the dark flies that salted her ass. Taking her tired body by the reins, he led her. It had been a long time, years, since men had tread on Valero.

Was he so degraded that they could look him in the eye and ridicule him?

He felt kinship with the beaten horse. Walking along, his anger intensified. He thought about his youth, about how there was a time in his life when no man would speak to him that way.

Had those days really passed?

You're sick, he reasoned. *You'll get better soon enough. You're sick.*

He patted the old mare's nose.

"You're a good gal," he whispered.

Valero decided he'd wait in Bone-of-Wellington a few days. He'd kill Frank if given the opportunity. Making good on the threat would make him feel better. The world needed less men like that anyway. He wondered if he'd kill the sheriff, too. He wished the young man hadn't insulted him. He was a good kid, and the world needed more men like that.

Perhaps, I won't, he thought.

It was a matter of redemption.

Frank was as good as dead, though.

MISERABLY, Felix Hines thrashed through the underbrush and entered a clearing. The sun was high overhead, and the day was exceedingly hot. Sweat covered his face and arms. His shirt was so damp it no longer wicked moisture. Thorns had ripped his hands. His skin was delicate—not that of a workingman. Dried blood caked his fingers. Here and there ticks dotted his body. He picked at the small, flat bugs, and a couple of them pinched away skin as he withdrew them.

He made too much haste in leaving the monastery. He'd been careless, wild, and he was ashamed.

Behind him there was no trail, and in front of him opened a large ravine. The brush and trees ended at the edge of a cliff. To step into the open was like being freed from a cage. There was a tropical feel to the air, with vines and creepers hanging from the trees and wrapping the trunks. Large ferns competed for space. Tangled roots erupted from the dirt.

Below his perch, the Kinnikinnick flowed. It was the same river that flanked the town, full of rolling timber there in a dammed section by the mill. Here the river flowed freely. The water was brown from the rain. The river was engorged, carrying debris from the forest.

Presently, the current whisked an entire tree, roots, leaves, and all, along its route. The tree crashed against a pile of rocks, twisted, and was, after a few broken limbs, on its way again.

Felix had to think. For him, there was nothing of which to be afraid. He had to find himself, and he had to be calm. He thought of the hammer in his grasp. He relived the moment with his father, the first impact, and he was strengthened.

It was nearly thirty feet from the cliff's edge to the water. Looking out, he felt like he'd escaped to the ocean. Kinnikinnick was that type of border. Felix was like Alexander, who wept when he reached the edge of the world. Felix read, too, about the salty air of the sea, which he guessed smelled quite different than the foul odor of this water. He decided that was where he'd go after he finished his business with Bone-of-Wellington. He'd visit the Pacific. It would be joyful to walk into the waves as the tide went out. Maybe he'd take a ship to China.

If the silver existed like Corbin promised, he'd have enough money to do whatever he pleased.

Shading his eyes from the sun, Felix gazed around. The river stretched ahead into a valley, and then the walls of adjoining hills enclosed it. He wondered if the Kinnikinnick flowed to the ocean. He had no idea how far he was from the Pacific. It could have been ten miles, a hundred, or a thousand.

The man from the monastery, the one who stole his horse, the one who left a rat-infested corpse in his wake, made no effort to follow. Felix was alone all day. He saw no sign of anyone on his trail. His moment of fear passed. Thinking about the corpse, Felix chuckled. He felt better, even curious. He wanted to see the cadaver again. The way the rat wedged into the open throat was particularly funny. He wondered if the rodent got stuck there, if it'd die like that, suffocating in the corpse's throat. That image got him laughing.

The body, the more he thought of it, made him think of a scarecrow, the shell of a man filled with stuffing. Even the vagabond rags were appropriate. After all, he mused, listening to the roar of the river, he'd seen no birds inside the monastery. There were plenty of birds at its fringe.

All this got him thinking of a ritual he attempted as a boy. There was a time in his life that he tried to conjure a devil in the Bone-of-Wellington graveyard. It was a preposterous thing, but what a sight he must have made. Pierce Ryder had a book on the history of witchcraft, with accounts of old grimoires, of necromancers, of possessions, of old hag witches and burnings. For a time, Felix was taken with the volume.

Felix didn't stop thinking about the corpse. It excited him. As a child, he would have tried to divine with a murdered man's body. He wished he still had that innocence. It would be fun.

After catching his breath, he turned from the ravine. The wall was rocky and steep, quite dangerous. There was no use trying to get to the water's edge. The ocean, wherever it lay, would wait. He moved back into the forest.

The posse from Bone-of-Wellington, if one formed, had yet to draw near. Maybe, Felix thought, it was fortuitous that dim-witted Maureen was stolen. She would have hindered him. She'd have kept him to the roads where men would search.

With a philosophical shrug, Felix retraced his steps.

A MAN inclined to the life of an itinerant (he was homeless for much of his life), he constructed the home for his bride. He had no other motive. He built the home for her, and he plowed the land for her. He went into town for her, and he came home at night for her. He did all these things, but, after the birth of their only child, a son she named Elijah, he couldn't stop the downward spiral of her mind.

He called it her retreat. Daily, she slipped away from him, drawing inward, listening to a voice that only she heard. She thought cancerous thoughts. She begged her husband to hear them, too. As a response, he simply touched her hair, kissed her skin.

It was the great tragedy of their lives.

"Do you not hear it?" she asked.

Then, when the answer was negative, she became irate, mean.

All the while, the child, Elijah, watched.

The most painful part of her decline was that she had moments of perfect clarity. Sometimes she'd emerge from the cloistered bedroom, doting on the men who took such wonderful care of her, manic in the love she gave. Her movements (elegant, the boy thought, and he'd remember it that way as a man) were musical. When well, she was a lovely woman. Life sparkled in her eyes.

Once, the boy listened as his father prayed. He asked his lord to keep her this way, to stop her sickness, but fog soon clouded her mind. She retreated. It became a recognizable pattern of behavior. She first became self-conscious, then quiet, then morose. Finally, holding back anger, she withdrew to the bedroom, closing the door. The lock would turn. Occasionally, she'd scream out at private ghosts. More often, though, as the boy pressed his ear to the door, all was silent within. Only when she shifted her position in the bed was the monotony broken.

When she caught him listening, she hurt him.

"I'm not your mother," she'd say, and then regale him with fantastic stories about his father, about how he was a killer. "I wouldn't fornicate with a dirty Mexican like your old man. I wouldn't soil myself for you."

The boy forgave her, but he grew resentful.

His father was more than resentful.

"If only she'd try," he'd say.

He even asked his son. "Why doesn't she try to change it?"

Towards the end of her life, she escaped the bedroom and walked the road to town. It was a two-mile stretch of dust, stone, and horse manure. The road winded through a patch of woods and lanced a cow pasture. Often, she made the journey in night clothes and bare feet. Sometimes she went in the early morning, and sometimes she trekked in the middle of the night. Whenever she went, she goaded fellow travelers (some of whom were neighbors, most of whom were strangers on horseback) with venomous reproaches. She no longer restricted the harangues to her son and husband. The insults became altogether Biblical, apocalyptic and puritanical. She had a penchant for calling the town to which she traveled, a tiny place on the Ohio River referred to as the South Shore, the Whore of Babylon.

Once, the boy followed and watched, keeping his distance, slipping between the trees. He wanted to protect his mother. That was his intention. Frightful men traveled the road away from the South Shore. Vicious drunks moving inland from the port. That night, the decision to follow her would be a decision that shaped the rest of his life.

Young Elijah Valero had taken his father's gun.

VALERO led the horse to a tributary of the river, a small vein barely wide enough to be a creek. Sunlight played across the brown water. The day was bright and hot. He navigated the flat, slick rocks with care. Finding a displaced boulder alone in a bed of sand, he took a seat.

Hunger gnawed at him. He wondered how he would find a meal in town, what type of work they'd put him through to earn a bite. He watched as a snake slithered away at the edge of the water. Briskly, no doubt perturbed, the serpent moved on. Valero considered shooting it and eating it, but he was too distracted for the task.

Greedily, the mare went to the water and dipped her head.

Poor gal, Valero thought, watching her.

She was unable to quench her thirst. Since leaving the monastery, she'd stopped to lap up every puddle in the road, no matter how crusted and scum-filled. She drank like she'd trekked across the desert. Valero did her the courtesy of emptying her saddlebags. The kid hadn't planned on going too far, apparently. He carried no food or anything useful for traveling. There were three books and a small journal. Valero had tossed the boy's things into a ditch.

In the distance, down the hillside towards Bone-of-Wellington, the peal of a hammer strike traveled upward. Rhythmically, each crack of the board resonated in the trees. Some carpenter was hard at work. Even in a place like this, life went on.

A breeze moved across the town in his direction, moved with the creek current. Chemicals and sawdust came with the wind. It was an odor that brought no nostalgia or sense of goodwill. Valero never had much luck in sawmill towns. He recalled one, a sore on the hide of the earth called Ellenwood, where he killed a drunken man who become too free with a rifle. The man carted the gun around like a six-shooter. He drank with the weapon on his lap. When drunk, he used it as a cane. The man, whose name Valero didn't recall, epitomized the problem with people in sawmill towns. The men were cooped up, worked too hard and too often, and there were no women, so they were always looking for a chance to prove themselves to one another. Sawmill towns functioned like tribes of animals. It wasn't enough to beat up on each other, either; they had to test their mettle on outsiders. In the end, Valero killed the man without pleasure. He was simply pushed to the point it became a necessary action.

He figured Bone-of-Wellington would be much the same as Ellenwood. His brief encounter with its inhabitants on the stage road didn't inspire a positive image.

Picking through the creek rocks, searching for something flat, Valero was glum. He dug his fingers into pale sand below the rock, where it was wet. He needed to stop thinking so much. As he traveled the road, he'd been dreaming while awake. More than dreaming, he dredged up memories older than Ellenwood. In fact, he'd unpacked his oldest memories. Memories of his mother.

The horse continued to drain the creek, oblivious and without worry. The wind brought more sawmill smells, which became more nuanced as one absorbed them.

At the back of Valero's mind, the barrage kept on.

His father said, *Why doesn't she try harder? Why can't she change? She knows what's wrong. Why doesn't she change? There isn't anything physically wrong.*

On and on, the same refrain. Valero understood his mother much better than he had as a child. He understood her more than his father ever did.

Valero exhumed a small rock as flat as a plate. Delicately, he cleaned off the sand until the face had gloss. His mother's and his father's grave markers, two thousand miles away, were nothing more than creek stones, larger but flat and smooth like this one.

A Baptist preacher, an old man with a paunch and a bald pate, not a good man, carved their names into the stones. Such was his duty. He placed a small cross on each of the stones, which was not his duty but made him feel better about the state of his parish.

Valero stood and tossed the rock into the current, where it sank below. He moved to the horse and patted her flank.

"Come on," he said. "That's enough. Let's get you home."

He clutched her reins.

———◆———

When he crested the small hillock, Bone-of-Wellington waited on the other side. He'd seen the town once before, when initially passing through. A glance was enough to make an impression. It was too ugly for him to stop then, and he experienced the same caution now. This was a small-scale version of cities back east, behemoths that coughed smoke and noxious fumes like Cincinnati and Pittsburgh. It hadn't their size and culture, though, only their scum.

One thoroughfare cut through the heart of the settlement. Even with the sun shining, the path was mud pocked by horses. A few buildings lined the street, poorly built, fashioned from the sawmill's discarded scrap. The residential islands of shacks that housed workers and their families stood like a second row of teeth behind the buildings of Main Street. The shacks were less organized, jutting in a rootlike system. The better homes were farther from the mill. The lesser homes lay in its shadow. On the far side of town, where the river flowed at a narrow juncture, stood the heart and soul of Bone-of-Wellington, a series of buildings that constituted the sawmill. Fresh logs from a logging camp upstream choked the restive, stinking river.

The lack of ornamentation, the absence of any decoration, struck Valero as a great contrast with the monastery he left behind. The monastery was built to inspire awe, whereas there was no pretense in the town below. This had been constructed out of necessity and nothing more. It was temporary. It was one of the most cynical places he'd ever seen.

At the bottom of the hill, grass ceased and mud began. The street ahead was empty. The haze of humidity looked like steam. The army surplus tents, of which there were many scattered between the buildings, shivered in the wind. It was the only movement Valero spotted. Smoke rose from a couple of the buildings, from inferno kitchens preparing giant meals for the workers. The aroma of porridge drifted to him on the wind. His mouth salivated. As he walked closer, the odor grew stronger, blotting out all else. The hunger was enough to drive a man to desperation.

The first building he came upon was more an open garage than a home or business. It was a shelter with three walls and a roof, fairly deep, and, at the back of it, an old man toiled. Sawhorses, laden with half-formed coffins, surrounded him. It was he who'd been doing the hammering. With the flick of his wrist, the man drove a nail into a slab of pine. He was so absorbed in his thoughts it would have been easy to sneak up on him without notice. Valero was in no mood for remaining concealed, however. Raising his hand in greeting, he moved to the entrance of the man's workshop. The smell of porridge was strong within, stronger than the sawdust and pine.

The man looked up, startled, and then he nodded. He placed an iron nail between his teeth, rolling it with his tongue as he stared. There was recognition in his eyes. He looked past Valero, scanning the familiar horse.

He was a man to whom years were unkind. He had bright, intelligent eyes, but all else was beaten down. His face was a mask of wrinkles, bags beneath his eyes, drooping cheeks, a permanently furrowed brow. His ears were unnaturally extended, and more hair grew inside them than around them. Of hair, he had little—grey tufts here and there.

Uncertain of the stranger (and with the morning's business who would blame him?), he kept his grip on the pin hammer as he slid between the coffins. He fetched a blue military cap from a peg on the wall, and he placed it on his head. The act did a great deal towards improving his form. No youth, maybe, but the cap gave him authority. If nothing else, he was less pitiful when he stood before Valero. He spat the nail into a trough of scrap.

"Pray tell, stranger. How'd you come by that horse?"

His eyes moved to the mare. Like a curtain, grief passed over his face.

"That's been explained to your sheriff," Valero said.

He was an obstinate cuss, pushy.

"We don't have a sheriff. He's a peace officer, and not even that if you want to go by the code of the law."

"Your pardon, old timer. It's been explained to the man with a tin badge on his chest."

"How 'bout the explanation in short? Just as courtesy." His knuckles whitened around the hammer shaft.

Hunger made Valero polite.

"In short, I found her. In short, I brought her back to the nearest town." Valero looked around. "If that's what you wanna call this place."

The old man nodded. "Stranger, you look like a starved dog."

"I keep hearin' that."

"Don't tell me you were takin' that road by foot. It's nothing but wilderness out here." He loosened his grip on the hammer.

Valero avoided the probing. "If you know this horse, why don't you stable her? She had a good drink earlier, but she needs food. Somebody put a good beating on her." He pointed. "Some salve wouldn't hurt those cuts, if you got any."

"Sure, stranger, I'll put her up. Her name's Maureen. She's a familiar gal around here. She's been at it a while."

Valero stroked her mane.

"Maureen," he said. He handed over the reins.

The old man placed the hammer in the scrap trough. He took Maureen and began to lead her off.

Before hitting the mud, he said, "There's a vat of gruel cookin' out back of the shed. Find you a bowl and help yourself. You look like you damn sure need it. About as much as Maureen needs it. Mind those three burlap bundles on the ground, though. Take my word for it. You don't wanna know what's in there."

"I'm grateful to you," Valero said. He meant it.

The old man smiled crookedly.

"Say that after you taste it. Go on," he said. "Help yourself."

SATIATED for the first time in months, Valero was lost in thought again, oscillating his gaze between the cauldron hung atop a fire pit and the three burlap sacks piled on a stretch of planks. The planks led through the mud to an outhouse and then to the back entrance of the building next door. The bowl, from which he'd consumed the gruel eagerly, lay empty before him.

Shaking off his thoughts, he stood and walked to the three bundles. There was, in the heat, the slightest stink rising from them. The old man had placed rose petals on two of the bundles, leaving the other austere and wet at the side with blood. The peace officer said the kid with the horse killed his family. This was the product. One of the bundles with a rose petal was quite small. A child, Valero presumed.

A settlement like this wasn't accustomed to seeing so much death. Aside from the occasional brawl or saw-mill accident, the place would be relatively safe. Murder, especially that of a child, would rattle the foundations of a town like Bone-of-Wellington. Valero wondered how many people would move because of this. He wondered if the settlement would survive.

The old man returned. He ambled around the side of the building, waving the steam of gruel from his face. Whatever he'd been doing, he'd worked up a sweat. His shirt was open at the neck, and the shirt was wet. He wicked the sweat on his brow. Along with Valero, he looked at the carefully arranged bundles.

"I didn't send you back here to get curious," he said.

"What happened?"

"You're lookin' at the Hines family. Deceased as of this morning." He pointed at the largest bundle. "His boy," he said. "He did it. Boy to me, but I guess he's a man. A man in age, anyhow."

Valero thought of the child at the monastery, wandering around, oblivious.

I could have shot him and saved these folks a lot of trouble, he thought. This wasn't his business, though, and he wasn't eager to make it his business.

"Tragedy," he mumbled.

The old man allowed the lame response.

"You ain't kiddin'," he said.

"No morgue here? No doctor to leave 'em with?"

"I'm the only doctor around. Before you say it, I know I don't look like a doctor. I'm not, but I know enough of the trade." He lifted the Union kepi from his head. "Learned on the job."

"I ain't ever seen a doctor that built coffins. Seems like a conflict of interest." Valero grinned.

"Builds coffins and digs graves. Only schoolteacher in these parts, too. Such is the plight of a man with half a brain. In the land of the blind, the man with one eye is king. I guess you heard that one."

"What's your name?" Valero asked.

"Pierce Ryder," he said. "Come inside a minute. I don't like to be glib in the presence of the dead. I still got the old respect about me. People these days don't respect shit."

Valero followed Ryder into the building next to the work shed. The sidewalk planks groaned under their steps.

"Besides," Ryder went on, "no reason to stand by that fire pit. It's hot enough."

He opened the back door, and a small dog, blonde and with a fat belly, sauntered out. The dog looked up at Valero, but it was unconcerned with his presence.

"That's Sophia," Ryder said. "She guards the place."

"Vigilant," Valero remarked.

Two windows at the front of the building allowed enough sunlight to make the place bright. It was a single room with an odd collection of items competing for space. There was a table with a blanket across it against the wall. Instruments of surgery hung on nails above the table. The blades looked like they participated in the war. They were well-used tools. An ominous leather pail waited beneath the table.

Two bookshelves, stuffed to brimming with leather volumes, occupied the other side of the room. Here, too, there were chairs and a dusty rug. Between the walls there were stuffed birds, paintings, a preserved military uniform, an old flag, a fiddle, a stack of journals, bells, a wind chime, and various Indian baubles. Atop one of the chairs was a Bible, its pages marked by a feathered Indian charm.

Noticing that Valero pondered the charm, Ryder said, "It's a sore spot with me that Indians don't walk these woods anymore. They did once."

Valero nodded tactfully. He'd never had much contact with Indians, only a few here and there who had already assimilated with whites.

"Say, stranger, why don't you offer your name? It ain't much to ask in return for a meal."

Ryder leaned his slight frame on the operating table. He pulled up a seat for his guest.

"Hell, to be frank, I'd like to know more about how you found that horse while you're at it."

"Elijah," he said.

"None more biblical than that."

"My mother's choice. She wouldn't argue with you."

Valero took the chair. It was good to be in a home with a living spirit rather than a dead one.

"What else?"

"Elijah Valero."

"I thought you had a tinge of Spanish in you. You got that coloring anyhow."

"My father," Valero said.

Ryder nodded. "How 'bout the horse?"

"You keep tobacco around?" Valero asked.

The old man rummaged in a drawer. He pulled out a pouch.

"A couple in there already rolled," he said.

Valero took it. Ryder lit one of the cigarettes. The smoke calmed him.

"That story hasn't changed. I found her."

"Where?"

The smoke kept him from growing perturbed. He exhaled through his nose.

After another draw, Valero said, "Up in the woods. At an old monastery."

Ryder crossed his arms. "Tell me this: did you hurt the boy?"

"That's the same thing your peace officer asked. Is that what y'all want?"

"Not me. I don't want that in the slightest."

Valero nodded at the back door.

"Not even with that?"

"No, not even with that."

"Well, I didn't hurt him. I saw him. He was alive. I left him that way. Or me and ol' Maureen left him that way."

"Why'd you take the horse?"

"You're the local detective, too."

"Just curious."

"He beat on that horse. It was either I take the horse or kill him for it."

"You'd kill for that?"

"Sure."

"But not for that?" He nodded to the back door, at the three bodies.

"That's different," Valero said. "I like horses."

"Looking you over, I presume you don't like hearin' people say they heard your name before."

Valero drew on the cigarette.

Ryder was admiring his possessions when Valero finally said, "I want to pay you back for the meal."

Ryder walked across the room and picked up the Bible. "As the Book says, 'Do not neglect to show hospitality to strangers, for thereby some have entertained angels unawares.' You don't owe anything, Mr. Elijah."

"It also says 'The wicked borrows but does not pay back.'"

Ryder raised his eyebrows. "You surprise me. You can read?"

Valero nodded. Smoke obscured his eyes.

Ryder laughed. "But damned if my mother wouldn't get pissed if folks quoted the Bible at one another while quarreling. You wanna eat again tonight, how 'bout you start by diggin' a grave? I can sure use the help. I'll show you where, and I'll show you how if need be. I got a shovel and pick in the shed. Ground's stony up there. You ever done work like that?"

"I've dug plenty of graves," Valero said.

Ryder looked him over. His eyes lost their gleam.

"I believe you have," he said.

HE moved swiftly past the columns of the solarium, sunlight blinking in and out. Felix was compelled to run. Intuition told him that a posse would arrive soon. He didn't like the odds of facing a posse with three bullets, especially with him being ignorant of his weapon. He made haste.

While walking in the woods an idea had come to him. There was something significant about the dead man, something that spoke to him on a profound level. Clearly, the scarecrow was left for his benefit. He should use it.

Fate, he thought, and he believed in fate.

He'd use the corpse as a scarecrow against the posse, that smug bastard Hector Bray and whomever he brought along.

Felix rushed through the front entrance and nearly leapt up the stairwell, taking three stairs at a time. He waded into a sea of rodents, parting them as he stomped the old wood. He paid no mind to the stench or buzzing flies. He kicked away rats and shoved his hand through a nest of maggots. He looked down into the open neck of the corpse. Indeed, the greedy rat had suffocated there. The rear end was high, but the tail sagged.

The man had a few teeth on one side of his jawbone. Most of the meat had been eaten away. Felix tugged at the body, gripping it at the shoulders, but it was cemented to the floor. He wrenched the corpse sideways, loosening it. Back and forth, he pushed and pulled. With every jarring of the corpse, maggots rained from the orifices. Angry, disturbed roaches scuttled out and wriggled their antennae.

With one great pull, he freed the corpse from the floor. In doing so, the waxen flesh of the thighs ripped free of the body and, as the torso lifted, blood thick as gruel, black blood, dumped out, spreading in a pool.

Despite the rats' protest, Felix dragged the corpse into the corridor and then toward the stairwell.

The garden was his destination.

Dragging the corpse by the ankle bones, Felix struggled through the weeds towards a muddy stretch of ground that dipped low and held rainwater.

Intermittently, a somber thought tainted his exhilaration. He hoped Corbin and Spence were clever enough to avoid the riders, to avoid the stage road entirely. His fear that they were never going to show—that perhaps they never intended to do so—remained. It was possible Corbin and Spence never meant any of the things they said to him.

What if they think me a fool? he wondered.

Felix struck that.

Time, he urged. *Have faith. Give them time.*

When he'd dragged the corpse to the wall, he stopped and released the ankles. Finding a suitable spot where vines grew thickly, Felix wedged the cadaver between their folds, enveloping it. He propped the body against stone.

Cleaning loose flesh from his hands, he stepped back to admire his work. The body was partially concealed, but it would be visible to anyone within five feet of it. Flies found it.

He wiped, but his hands wouldn't be cleaned. Where the maggots had yet to erupt, the body was, like a snake, shedding its outer coat, revealing a new, waxy layer of skin below. On his palms, the flesh rolled and crumbled as he brushed it. Felix used his trouser legs for the task, but it was futile.

Satisfied, he traced his steps back through the solarium.

It was then that Felix heard riders in the distance. He heard the beating of hoofs. When voices followed, his heart lurched. He pulled the revolver from his trousers and sprinted towards the kitchen. There was a door in the back wall. Breathless, he opened the door and emerged outside, in the back of the monastery. A sloping hill led towards a stand of forest. Outside, he heard the riders louder. The men were in the front garden. He sprinted down the hill towards the safety of the trees. Once beyond the wood line, he stopped, breathing heavily, holding the gun without aiming.

That's when he saw a dark figure, a man even deeper in the woods, watching him. From this distance, he was only a shadow. Felix's heart arrested. He went cold. With a clumsy gesture, he changed his grip on the revolver, spreading loose skin on the walnut handle.

The man, rail thin, did not move nor speak. Felix imagined he held a gun, a rifle at his side. Felix swallowed nervously. Sweat gathered at his hairline, and a touch of nausea passed through his gut.

The voice, when it came from behind, nearly made him faint.

"That's cuttin' it damn close," the man said.

HECTOR Bray found himself alone, guiding his horse through what had been a vegetable garden. From the top of the hill, the layout of the fields was visible. Squat firs grew in the fields, young trees. Underbrush—weeds high as a man's waist—dominated what remained. A taller forest rose at the bottom of the slope, while the monastic ruins stood high at the top.

The day was hot, but the air moved. Hector removed his hat to let his head cool in the breeze. The horse, tired and bored, sauntered into the cooler shadow of the ruins and chewed at the grass. Hector let the animal wander, resting his arms on the saddle horn.

Like most folks in town, he'd visited the ruins in the past. He and Constance, one Sunday five months prior, made the trek. It was late winter then, and a light snow fell over the battlements. Constance thought the grounds romantic, but Hector found the place dreary and unsettling. Ryder had filled her mind with stories about the monastery. Ryder knew its history better than anyone, and he'd relate it in detail to anyone who cared to listen.

Constance insisted on going inside, despite Hector's caution. She marveled at the snow falling through holes in the chapel ceiling, and even he admitted the scene was beautiful. Winter gave the ruins a touch of romance, perhaps, but summer exposed the melancholy bones of the place.

Currently, birds infested the grounds, swarming like they do during a cicada summer. A few trees at the corner of the field were black with birds, and a murder of crows lined the top of the monastery like gargoyles. The birds crossed the fields, lifting from one tree to go weigh down another. The limbs shook with them.

The scene was unsettling.

Hector wished Ryder had come along. He'd welcome the old man's talk of omens, augury being another of his many trades.

If Felix had been at the monastery, as the man who called himself Valero claimed, he was not here now. The man could have lied, but the fact that he possessed the Hines' family horse made his claim difficult to ignore. Valero might be a liar, or he might, if the rumors were true, believe things that weren't true. He had a reputation for being off-kilter. If the stories were to be believed, he was not only a killer, but Eli Valero was also a dangerous lunatic.

Where Felix went was anybody's guess. Although it troubled Hector, he had no energy to search farther afield. He wanted to be home with Constance. With the sun past its apex, the day waning, she'd be deeply worried about him. He hoped fear wouldn't hurt the baby.

Could it?

Dejectedly, he thought of the hours-long ride the posse faced even if they returned to Bone-of-Wellington this instant.

Once Tom Parker and his crew showed, the men would insist on camping here for the night. A couple of the men brought whiskey. They were enjoying themselves. Grief and outrage had nothing to do with their presence.

"Get up," he said, nudging the horse to head up the hillside.

Where the hell is Parker?

He hoped the kid hadn't been bullied into something stupid.

I shouldn't have put him in charge.

Make up your mind, Hector chided. *Either you want Felix lynched, or you want to do right. It's black and white. You can't sit in between.*

"Hey there!"

Startled, Hector looked around. On the first story of the monastery, hanging out one of the windows, Frank Wolf and his boy whistled for attention. Shadow partially masked their faces.

"Tom and the boys are headin' up the trail," he said. "About a quarter mile down."

"Get out here then," Hector shouted. "We'll meet 'em out front."

———•◆•———

What changed?

Hector watched Tom Parker, who had scaled the front wall. He sat with his legs dangling against the chalky stone. Parker was taciturn, watching the garden from his high perch. He and Hector were the only men who sought to be alone. The others toiled in the garden, clearing space for a fire pit. They had already sampled the whiskey.

Over Parker's shoulder, the sun was sinking. Dusk moved in with a bank of clouds. Hector rested his back against a column. He took great care with the cigarette he smoked, having rolled it with delicate patience. Tobacco wasn't dear (he brought plenty along), but something inside told him to enjoy it. He inhaled, letting the smoke get deep into his lungs.

A bat, freshly awakened, darted through the solarium. In the bushes at his side, fireflies winked. Lightning bugs, as Constance called them. There was no shortage of mosquitoes in the air, either, but cigarette smoke kept them distant.

The world was askew. Again, the question came to mind.

What changed? Why did he feel like this smoke would be his last?

Parker watched the forest.

It occurred to Hector that Alf ordered Tom to climb the wall. The kid used the perch as a crow's nest.

They feel it, too, Hector thought.

The cigarette burned closer to his fingers. He took another draw, and then he let the stub burn. Looking up at the monastery in the waning light, with shadows filling the chipped crevices, a distinct chill went through his body. Although none of the men would admit it, there was a reason they camped in the courtyard rather than within the old walls of the ruins. The towering structure frightened them. Night made the monastery a different place.

"No, bigger than that," one of the men shouted, walking the contour of the fire pit. "This has to be a big-ass fire. I mean *big*."

"Yeah, I don't want no piddly-ass fire," another said.

Me neither, Hector thought. *Keep the dark at bay. He finished the cigarette.*

WITH care spawned of boredom rather than pride, Valero stood in the grave, concealed to his chest. He used the shovel to make the walls slick and straight. Sinking four feet into the earth, and spanning six feet in length, it was a nice grave. Beige clay in the soil gave the walls a shine, especially when a beam from the waning sun hit.

On a bank above a flood plain, with the scent of reeds, fish, and river water in the air, Valero toiled in the cemetery, earning his gruel. With the back of the shovel, he packed the walls tighter, making a circuit from the head of the grave to the foot and then back again. A pile of dirt and stone stood beside the hole. Ryder's ancient pick lay in the grass.

Grave markers surrounded Valero. There were embossed stones and flat rocks from the riverbed, none of which were pleasing to the eye. There was no shortage of wood in town, so a cross two feet high topped each plot. Some of the crosses were cockeyed, weatherworn.

It struck Valero that the three new graves made the fenced wedge of land crowded. Outside the back fence there were a few animal graves, but soon Ryder would have to remove the fence and extend the cemetery. When he did, animals and people would rest together.

As it should be, Valero thought.

Valero lifted the shovel and placed it on the rim. He'd earned a few meals, he figured. After cracking his tired bones, he hoisted himself from the grave. With his boots in the hole, he sat on the grass.

He was contemplating the purchase of a horse when the creak of a wagon drew his attention. The scent of fresh pine preceded Ryder. When Valero turned to see, the old man doffed his cap. He moved up the incline of the graveyard path, pulling the cart like a mule.

A fair woman walked in Ryder's shadow, pretending to be oblivious to the stranger with his feet in the grave. She watched the river to her left. She was a tall woman, a couple inches taller than Ryder, and there was elegance in her gait. Her clothes were old rather than fine, but the dress fit her shape well enough that most would ignore the age of the fabric. Valero sensed her magnetism as she approached. He barely glanced at the old man.

"Fine, fine, fine," Ryder was saying.

He lowered his cart to the grass, and the coffin atop it shifted, sliding against the guard with an unsettling thud. He walked the contour of the grave, nodding with satisfaction.

Valero watched the woman until he caught her eye. She looked over him like she'd look over a pile of refuse, a quick glance, necessary but without enjoyment.

Self-consciously, he wiped sweat from his face. The rag came away brown with filth.

Starved dog, indeed.

"Hello," Valero mumbled.

Ryder cleared his throat.

"This is Constance Bray," he said. "Wife of our peace officer. That'd be Hector, the man you met on the trail. Constance, this is Elijah Valero."

"How do you do," she said.

Again, she looked at the river rather than the man before her. She was nervous.

Her good looks made Valero nervous, too. Her dark hair, pulled back severely, framed the lovely bones of her face. Her wandering eyes were brown.

"That's the baby girl," Ryder said, nodding at the coffin. "She isn't heavy, but I'd appreciate help gettin' her down without breakin' the box."

Valero stood.

"No ceremony?" he asked.

He wiped his dirt-crusted palms on the corduroy of his trousers. He looked towards town, but he found no sign of a procession. Only Constance Bray followed Ryder to see the deed done.

Such a burial wasn't fitting for a man, let alone a child.

"You're lookin' at it," Ryder said. "Go ahead, little miss."

Constance snatched a handful of wildflower petals from the pouch at the front of her apron. Somberly, she parted her hands over the grave and allowed the petals to fall like water through the crease. The colorful array fell without grace, dumping in a pile. After rummaging, she pulled a few more petals and tossed them one by one towards the head of the grave.

Valero removed his hat.

"Nobody cared to come pay respects?" he asked, quieter now, as if to not interrupt the woman and her flowers.

"There's work to be done," Ryder said. "We had the sacks out in the street this morning. Most of the men came by with their wives. It wouldn't do to wait for the men on the trail to get back to put 'em in the ground. Too hot."

"Let's pray," Constance said. She eyed Ryder.

Bowing their heads, they prayed silently.

Valero thought of the monastery and the chapel in which he'd spent so much time. In the stillness, insects buzzed around the coffin.

When finished, Ryder said, "I got the box hooked up to leather thongs. You and me should be able to get it down that way."

It was simple enough. The coffin was disturbingly light. Without strain, he and Ryder lowered the box into the hole. Then, with a yank, Ryder retrieved the strips of leather. Constance threw a handful of dirt, thick with the beige clay, onto the lid of the coffin. Pebbles sounded like hail against a rooftop.

Ryder offered a pinch of dirt.

"Ashes to ashes," he said.

"Mr. Valero," Constance said, "may I ask you something?"

Valero, placing his hat on his head, looked at the woman. He grabbed his coat from the grass. Dirt had dried in the lines of his knuckles.

"Did Hector seem under duress when you saw him?"

"How do you mean?"

"The peace officer," Ryder reminded him. "The man with the badge."

"Did he look like he was in control?"

Valero considered.

"He didn't look like he was in trouble," he said, "if that's how you mean. He was doin' what was expected of him. He was leading a search."

"So, he was in charge?"

"He rode out front."

"What she means," Ryder interjected, "is whether or not that posse was draggin' him around."

"He seemed capable enough," Valero said, although he didn't mean it.

Constance turned from Valero.

"I worry about him so," she said. She touched a pendant attached to a necklace of silver. It was an old piece of jewelry. Valero wondered if it were an heirloom, or if her husband had gifted it to her. She remained clutching the pendant as she started back on the slope towards the bevy of shacks.

"Ma'am," Valero called. "Your old man looked tough to me. He'll be fine."

She didn't stop or turn.

Mesmerized, Valero watched her go.

Ryder cracked his back, and then he hoisted the shovel. He pushed his cap to the crown of his head.

"We'll get the other two in the ground tomorrow," he said, "but I'd like to get this girl underneath before dark."

With that, the first shovelful of dirt rained down, splashing across the pine.

With Constance out of earshot, Valero said, "He looked like he had a bull by the horns."

"Hector?" Ryder punched the shovel into the mound of dirt.

Valero nodded.

"Fair assessment, I'd guess. Sad thing about it is he's off the job as of next week. Talk about gettin' a customer just before you close."

"Fired?"

"No, nobody willin' to do that piss-poor job would get fired. He was takin' the old lady to California. You can't see it in her figure, but she's with child."

"Damn shame."

Valero took the spare shovel from Ryder's hand-drawn cart. He drove it into the middle of the pile and dirt cascaded from the top. He tossed a shovelful into the open hole

"I don't think he's in much danger of harm," Ryder said. "Nobody's taken the time to thump him yet. He may get his conscience bruised, though. I worry about that more than anything. If they find Felix alive, they'll string him up. Hell, they'll beat the kid until there's not an unbroken bone in his body. I hate the thought of it. Hector, I think he hates the thought of it, too. He'll try to do right. Just a matter of how much he's willin' to put himself between those fellas and Felix. To what degree he'll take a stand."

"Ain't a good position for the righteous man," Valero said.

Ryder nodded. "Or the dutiful one."

Earth covered the length of the coffin, and the holes around its contour began to fill. Maybe it was fatigue but putting dirt back into the hole was more difficult than shoveling it out. Valero mashed a mosquito against his forearm. Dusk was alive with mosquitoes flying inland from the river. The sky clouded and grew dark.

"Where'd the day go, huh?" Ryder asked.

He rested on his shovel like a crutch. He pulled a tobacco pouch from the pocket of his vest.

Valero continued to shovel.

"Did Mrs. Bray know this girl?" he asked.

"Sure," Ryder said. "Everybody knows everybody here." He licked the paper of the cigarette and closed it tightly. He patted his vest for a match. "Constance helps me teach these kids a little readin' and writin'. She's smart as they come. You know, this girl here, Willa Hines, I delivered her into this world."

"Mrs. Bray help you there, too?"

"Constance ain't been here but less than a year. Willa Hines was eight years old. You got children, Elijah?"

"Not any I'm aware of," Valero said.

"I used to." Ryder struck the match and lit the cigarette. The tip glowed orange.

Valero took a drag when it was offered. The smoke felt good. With some reluctance, he handed back the cigarette.

"There isn't anything in this world more depressing than burying a kid," Ryder said.

Balancing the cigarette between his lips, he rejoined Valero at the diminishing pile of dirt. Bats streaked across the air, chasing the mosquitoes.

After a period of silence, Ryder said, "Constance will have a supper for us." Even in the waning light, Valero noticed that his eyes were wet with tears. "Hell of a thing," he kept saying. "Hell of a thing."

There was nothing much more to say.

Death's always a hell of a thing, Valero thought. *Sometimes it's a shame, too.*

The men shoveled and scraped until the grave heaved with overturned soil.

— ◆ —

At dinner that night, sitting around a table in Pierce Ryder's home, Valero listened as the old man and Constance talked of Hector, his bravery and misfortune. If they were looking to impart reverence for the young man, they were unsuccessful. Valero found their chatter tedious. Men like Hector neither impressed nor moved him. He'd seen many of Hector's kind, men who called pride duty, and who mistook an unwillingness to displease for character. If he were foolish enough to take on a job like peace officer in Bone-of-Wellington (for the reward of a few dollars), then who could feel pity for him? Besides, Valero had found him to be a smartass.

Valero was full, at least, and so was the dog, Sophia, curled at his feet. Supper was more than he expected. He stuffed himself on bread and chicken. Ryder even served a couple mugs of frothy beer. As the voices of his companions droned on, Valero watched the traffic of men on the street moving to and from a spot called Rand's. He drew on a small cigar.

Ryder had told him Rand's Hotel and a whore shack by the river were the hubs of existence in town. Men stopped at Rand's before work and after work, and then again after a stop at the shack. It was a buffer between home and the mill. Only a few of the workers had families.

A kerosene lamp burned on the windowsill of Ryder's home. As the night grew darker, the men outside faded and only the reflections of three faces, the lamp, and tallow candles atop the bookshelves, filled the black pane.

"Elijah, you willin' to do some more work tomorrow? I can use you." Ryder blew a cloud of smoke.

Constance watched the smoke longingly. She was too modest to partake in the company of men. She tried to inhale the cloud, the way she leaned closer. Odd that she didn't find dining with two men, and neither one her husband, immodest. Such was the liberality of a woman removed from the east. Constance was raised in Cincinnati. Valero nearly told her that he grew up beside the Ohio River, but he'd only be talking at her and not to her. He found Constance an enigma.

"For a bed I would," Valero said. He exhaled smoke.

"How 'bout a bed and another round of meals tomorrow? Agreeable?"

Valero nodded. He took a drink of warm beer. The food had gone to his head more than the alcohol. He experienced a great fatigue, a heaviness that weighted his limbs. The past months collided with him. He was emotional at the prospect of another day like this, even if it meant digging graves with a wistful old man.

Constance noticed the change, because she turned her attention to Valero for the first time that night.

"How is it," she asked, "that a man of your nature ended up here?" She regarded him with suspicion. "You're not acquainted with Felix Hines, are you?"

Valero didn't respond. He blew cigar smoke in her direction.

"He robbed Felix of his horse," Ryder said, chuckling. He reclined in the chair, letting the cigarette burn between his fingers.

Valero took another drink of beer.

"Ol' Maureen."

With sass, Constance said, "That's a crime, too."

"Your husband excused my error in judgment. Said he'd forgive if I brought her back. A lenient man, Mr. Bray."

"I'm still curious as to what brought a man of your nature to Bone-of-Wellington."

"What nature is that?"

Constance scoffed. "We'll just ignore the obvious, I suppose."

"For a time," Valero said simply, "I was unwell. This is where I ended up. For a time before that I was down in the Rockies. A beautiful country, which this isn't."

Ryder offered Constance his cigarette. "Eye it any harder and it'll shrivel in my hand," he said.

She took it and put it between her lips indelicately. She looked at the window, at her reflection, as she took a draw.

"In public, she acts like she doesn't do those things," Ryder said.

With a gulp, he finished the beer before him. He winked at Constance, who didn't offer to return the cigarette, and he laughed some more.

"You know what I mean," Constance said. "You're a killer, aren't you? A murderer."

"Connie," Ryder cautioned.

Valero looked in her eyes.

"Sometimes," he said.

What else was there to say? She thought what she thought, and half of it was true.

"It's men like you that got Hector into trouble."

Valero took the abuse.

He asked, "What brings a woman of your upbringing to Bone-of-Wellington?"

"A stubborn man," she said. Enveloped in smoke, she smiled sardonically. "There was a time when I thought we were going to bed down and be on our way with the next stage."

"Is Hector a righteous man?" Valero asked.

Constance frowned. "No, he isn't *righteous*." She disliked the word. The smoke issuing from her mouth stuttered as she laughed. She looked at Ryder knowingly. "I think he's afraid of California is all."

"Hector is a good man," Ryder countered. "So is Elijah, Connie."

Constance raised her eyebrows. "What about you, Pierce?" she asked. "May as well bare your soul."

"A man with rotten luck," Ryder said. "I've been here thirteen years, believe it or not. As long as the mill."

"What was the rotten luck?" Constance asked.

Ryder sighed. He placed paper on the table and began to roll another cigarette.

"I knew old man Argo when he was still in Utah. My rotten luck was that I trusted his forked tongue. He's a bastard. You don't get money like he's got without bein' a bastard. You know he thought Bone-of-Wellington was going to be like Seattle?"

"You're kidding?" Constance stubbed out the cigarette with a practiced motion.

Ryder put up his hand.

"Honest to God. He thought it'd be a hub where all the trains crossed. He thought that shit river would be another Missouri River."

"Now a train comes through every two weeks."

"Just because I got a reputation for bein' bright doesn't mean I am actually bright. I bought what Argo said. I believed him."

Constance shook her head.

"I have no room to talk," she said. She stood then. Despite her words, her countenance took a morose turn. "Gentlemen, if you'll excuse me." She forced a smile. "Mr. Valero, I apologize for being rude."

Ryder stood politely, but Valero nodded from his seat. He had no room for decorum, especially in the face of insincerity.

Constance went out the door and started into the dark street.

"Shouldn't we escort her?" Valero asked.

"Isn't that type of town," Ryder said.

Valero reached down and nudged Sophia awake. He lifted the sleepy dog into his lap.

"How 'bout you escort her," he told the dog.

Sophia yawned, and then she settled her chin in the crook of Valero's arm.

The irony of Ryder's statement caught up with him.

Self-consciously, he added, "Well, it didn't used to be that type of town."

WHEN Felix turned and saw the face of Corbin Blum, he dropped the revolver in relief. The weapon fell to a bed of dead leaves. An incredible weight lifted from his chest. He wasn't alone. He wouldn't have to face the posse by himself. More deeply, he was relieved that he hadn't been betrayed. Corbin and Spence rewarded his trust. From the etiquette he learned from men like Corbin, however, he hid his elation behind a stolid mask. He did not, as he wanted to do, step forward and embrace the man with open arms. Rather, he stood by the fallen gun and looked on, as if he'd expected the man to be standing there all along.

Corbin was a tall man, lean and sinewy, with a terribly large Adam's apple that drew attention from his gaunt and scarred face. He had one eye that worked and moved. The other, slit by a blade, was white and clouded, shrunken and stationary. His sockets sank far enough into his flesh that it gave the appearance of black crescents above his cheeks. He had longs ears and a long, slightly hooked nose, and sandy hair tousled like that of a child. He wore a grey hat that looked like several men before him had worn it. There was something disappointing in his visage, something that conflicted with the Corbin of Felix's memories. The burden of hardship and ill luck blotted any air of prosperity. It was apparent that Corbin had been living roughly.

"Kid," he said, "it's damned good to see you." He spoke quietly, and he glanced around for any movement. "Spot of luck findin' you. We watched that monastery for an hour."

Raising his arm, he beckoned Spence forward. At his signal, his partner came out of hiding, crushing weeds, cradling his rifle like a hunter.

"It's a relief to see you," Felix admitted. He knelt and grabbed his revolver from the leaves.

Spence stepped into the clearing. "Felix," he said with a nod. "How goes it?"

Spence Hickman cast an image quite different than that of his partner. He was a man built for brawling, with heavy shoulders and chest, and a jaw that looked like it was cut from granite. He had craggy, pocked skin from a childhood bout with smallpox, scars he attempted to conceal beneath a dark mustache and patch of beard on his jaws. Unlike most, he kept his hat hanging on his back with a rope knotted at the front of his neck, not unlike a Mexican with a sombrero. On his corded forearm, which he left exposed with a shirt rolled to the elbow, he displayed a faded Navy tattoo of a devil lancing a heart (a relic of which Felix knew little). His countenance, regardless of the moment, retained its fierceness. Even at rest, his face was angry, his brow drawn. There was something primitive in the shape of his skull.

Corbin stared at the flesh and grist on Felix's hands, arms, and trousers. He framed his question with typical irreverence.

"Don't tell me that's from your old man?"

"Jesus Christ," Spence said. He sneered and spat a gob of tobacco juice.

Felix shook his head.

"It's nothing," he said. "A scarecrow I set up for the posse. My father's back in town with the others."

"The others? Who else did you bag?"

Felix shrugged.

"My Ma and Willa," he said.

Spence let out a low whistle of admiration. He raised his eyebrows.

"You killed your Ma? I'll be damned."

"Cold as a goddamn cat," Corbin agreed. "No wonder you got 'em riled. Who's that then?" He nodded at the residue. He wouldn't let it go. In some ways, Corbin was a careful man.

"Some old dead bastard on the top floor. Had his head blown off. He'd been there a while."

Spence sharpened his gaze. "What do you mean? You serious?"

Felix nodded.

"You found a dead man, and you didn't do it?"

"I didn't do it. I pulled him out in the garden for those boys to find. Give them a good scare. They might think it's a monk from the monastery," he said.

He looked at Corbin, hoping for a laugh. Spence never laughed at anything.

Corbin smiled.

Spence said, "Shit, we passed—" He stopped then.

Corbin said, "Couldn't have been that asshole tramp."

Felix was left out, so he asked Corbin, "Remember when you used to tell me about your gallows days?"

"Sure."

"I always liked the idea of that," he said. "You think that was a good prank?"

Corbin laughed.

"Sure, kid. You'll have plenty more to play with in a couple days."

"Bunch of disgustin' assholes," Spence said. "Christ."

"We're gonna need to get deeper into the woods for the time bein'," Corbin told Felix. "Gotta wait it out till dark."

"Goddamn miracle they didn't spot you," Spence interjected. "Hope your scarecrow don't run 'em off either."

"Don't look like they're in a rush," Corbin said. "Hopin' they camp down for the night. We'll follow 'em wherever they do. I'm hopin' it's right fuckin' here."

"Campin' out at the base of the wall," Spence said. "Right out in the open. Be like a damned firing squad."

"We counted twelve earlier. Sheriff is with 'em. Bennie Wolf is with 'em, too." Corbin smiled again. "I figured you'd enjoy that, kid."

A surge of excitement passed through Felix. It was enough to make his heart race.

"Tell me this," Spence said. He paced back to Felix and Corbin. "Old man Argo and his gang haven't been through since we left, have they?"

"Yeah, I was wantin' to ask the same," Corbin said.

"I've been watching for him," Felix said. "There isn't any silver been taken out of Bone-of-Wellington. If it's ever been there, it's there now."

"I told you it's there," Spence said.

Chastised, Felix nodded.

"It's there," he said.

Spence's stare lasted too long for comfort.

Finally, he said, "Let's head back in here. We got a wagon and food. We'll get 'em soon as it's night."

"Fuckin' ducks on a pond," Corbin said.

After a spell of silence, during which they traversed a hundred yards of underbrush, and during which dusk approached, Corbin gave another smile to Felix and patted him on the back.

"You excited, kid?" he asked.

"I'm just damned glad to see you," Felix said.

HECTOR sat away from the others, on the stony earth with his back against the wall. Clouds had passed through, and stars were out. It was a beautiful night, warm and still. The monastery's silhouette became more familiar as the hours went by. Smoke from the campfire, around which the men drank and chattered, drifted into the trees, breaking apart in the leaves and swirling into the sky.

Watching the changing shapes of the smoke could mesmerize a man or send him to a deep place of thought. It had had the latter effect on Hector. Snippets of talk drifted to him. The men had lost all tact with the first bottle of whiskey. Frank Wolf cited Hector's dawdling as the reason they'd yet to snare Felix. He looked at the peace officer as he spoke.

Hector listened, but he didn't bite.

Staring into the flames, a memory of Constance came to Hector and made him smile. At a train station in St. Louis, with banks of steam obscuring the sea of faces, Constance broke his grip with the twist of her arm. She shouldered through the fellow passengers, her mouth a hard line of determination. To Hector's astonishment, she climbed a rack of luggage. There she stood atop trunks like a mountaineer on a ledge above the clouds. Before one of the porters shooed her away, Constance looked out, admiring the view. She shaded her eyes.

With this view of his precocious wife, guilt intruded. Hector had done Constance a great disservice by remaining in Bone-of-Wellington. She wanted California. He promised it to her.

After the luggage incident, when he regained the clutch of her hand, she said she had hoped to see California in the distance.

"What'd you see?" he'd asked.

"The edge of civilization," Constance had said. "The vast ocean of it." Free of the crowd, she kissed his cheek. As though she were demure, she'd whispered, "California was on the other side."

Oh, Felix couldn't get far. I'd say he's off in those woods, cowering, pissing his pants at the thought of us so close.

He's a smart kid. I still think we should have followed the train tracks.

If he hops a train, he's gone for good.

Just like Hector would want it. Ain't that right, Bray?

You're an asshole, Frank.

Say that to my face.

How much closer do you want me to get?

Y'all need to shut the hell up. I swear to God I keep hearing something rustle in the weeds.

You old fool, you can't hear half the shit that's said to your face, let alone somethin' outside a damn wall.

That's selective deafness. Meaning when I don't wanna hear a prick like you speak, I don't.

Privilege of being an old man is me not smashin' your teeth.

By God, I'm serious. If you'd listen a second, you'd hear it. There it is again.

Bray, you hear somethin'?

Hector?

The peace officer stirred. "What's that, old timer?"

"Somebody out there."

Hector sighed. He had to piss anyway.

"I'll take a look," he said.
"Big man. Look at him."
Chasing shadows, Hector thought.

THE boy, clutching the oversized gun with two hands, mentally running through the steps his father had taught him, steps that preceded squeezing the stiff trigger, stalked the creek bed that led alongside the road to South Shore. His mother was too lost in her thoughts to notice the boy's proximity. Clad for sleep, she walked mostly in silence, brooding, her rage growing, occasionally stopping to berate some unseen figure in the darkness. She clutched her fists and threw them.

Elijah had the wild idea of protecting his mother. His father had lost his feeling for her, no longer fighting to stop her excursions. As he had done for a long time, Elijah's old man slept in a different room than his wife. He was asleep, oblivious. He'd been in an alcohol-induced sleep when Elijah took the gun.

The dark figure, a sight Elijah would never forget, came riding.

At first, his mother jumped to the side of the road in fright. The rider passed with so much haste he was a blur, a wisp of shadow. Elijah fumbled with the gun, preparing the weapon. Wind made the revolver cold as ice. The boy's fingers were hard.

His mother targeted the man with a choice remark, something venomous the boy didn't quite understand.

The rider and horse jolted to a stop. The pair turned.

From the creek, Elijah saw the frost of the horse's breath, great clouds that issued as the animal snorted. The rider bent at the waist, and he pulled something from his saddlebag.

The boy's bellicose mother stomped and shouted.

With elegance, the horse stepped closer. The master of the horse, a Hangman, had a noose draped over his shoulder. He showed the loop in the moonlight.

BOOK THREE
"NIGHT MUSIC"
BEING AN ACCOUNT OF
SCARECROWS AND ABERRATIONS.

VALERO awoke in the darkness, a film of cool sweat on his body. With the dream fresh in his mind, he listened for hoofs against dirt and gravel. The loft was silent, as was the workshop below it and the street outside. Only the chatter of crickets and frogs from the river bottom came to him.

He was disoriented, wrapped in darkness, alone in a strange place.

The pile of hay he used for a pillow was no longer a comfort. The straws were like needles prodding his neck. He'd gone to sleep feeling safe, but the feeling left him. His back was stiff and his arms sore. Although he'd never admit it, he was in no shape for the labor he endured. The muscles of his hands ached from gripping the shovel, so much so that it was painful to open and close them. He couldn't remember the last time making a fist caused him pain. If his skin wasn't hard as leather, he'd have raw palms.

A damp chill pervaded the air. The cold made him shiver. Valero rolled from the hay and rose to a sitting position. He crossed his arms for warmth. He watched the triangular opening to his right, an empty space small enough for cats, which opened onto the street. Fog, thin as stretched cotton, snaked inside. Planks groaned as Valero crawled towards the opening. He dashed the fog and looked out. There was nothing to see save for more fog, a heavy bank of which filled the street and shrouded buildings. In the distance, from one of the eaves, a wind chime of old pie plates made subtle music.

He was frustrated, and he was cold down to his bones. Putting his back against the angled ceiling, he pulled his knees to his chest for warmth. Valero felt old.

An unwelcome memory came to him. It was an intrusion. He lowered his head in regret and shame. Vividly, he saw the old man, whose name he never learned, walking in the darkness toward the monastery. He'd been so starved he'd eaten raw rats.

He was, Valero thought, *a man who suffered. I killed him. He was terrified.*

He relived the firing of the gun, the jolt in his hand, the shock in his wrist. The first shot busted the old man's skull. His legs folded as if they were boneless. More shots followed, leaving the man with nothing in place except his jawbone, and even that cracked with the concussion of the shots.

The fog, which he'd scattered, resumed its shape around Valero's legs.

I thought he was the Hangman.

You know where you belong, Valero thought. *There are places for the sick. Your mother should have been taken away and locked in one of those cells. You would have visited her.*

How many now? How many have you killed? How many undeserving?

Valero counted by placing a finger against his knee, brushing away the crust of mud as he did. There was the soldier. There was the boy. His stomach twisted with the pinch of a talon. There was the bounty hunter. There was young Liza, with whom he nearly fell in love. She explained away Valero's fits by calling them night terrors. In hindsight, she was as bad as his father, unable to face the truth. He couldn't bear to think of her any further.

Darkly, the image of Liza with her throat bleeding came to him.

Valero sobbed. He hadn't cried in a long time, and the tears were like a release from months of pain.

Wiping his hands (brutish, inelegant hands like those of his father) across his face, he thought again: *There are places for the sick.*

He looked to the loft's opening, to where the gibbous moon made the fog glow. To his horror, the Spider hung from the eave. The black arachnid, large enough that the hair on its legs was visible, clutched a dying moth. The moth, a light green, twitched its wing in resistance, yet it was too weak to stop the Spider from entwining it.

Valero crawled forward on his knees, watching the Spider, wondering how she'd escaped his view before. Then he thought of how she materialized from a stone wall in the monastery, how she oozed like sap from a tree.

She manifested without reason.

Please, he thought. *Not now. Please.*

He closed his eyes, steeling himself. Like his father, he tried to wish away the sickness.

When Valero opened his eyes, the Spider had gone, as had her struggling moth.

The moment left him with a lyric, softly in the tone of his mother.

Dig a grave, dig a grave in the meadow.
Dig a grave in the cold hard ground.
Dig a grave, dig a grave in the meadow.
Gonna lay Darlin' Corey down.

Did she sing it the night she died? Had she sung it at all?

Puzzled, watching for the vanished Spider, watching the fog, Valero tried to turn his mind to other things.

Amid his wondering, nestled against the image Ryder's dog Sophia, came a foreign voice.

Be careful lest you dig your own grave, the Spider said.

Tomorrow he'll have you dig a grave the perfect size, Elijah. As you do, the old man will prepare your coffin. What better task for a Hangman?

The Spider, with the moth wrapped so tightly it was motionless as death, lowered into the fog. In the cone of moonlight, the Spider folded her legs in on herself and then stretched large again. It looked like a clenching fist.

Valero covered his face like a child.

Fight it, he thought. *It's too soon. She doesn't come this often.*

The Hangman's a-comin', the Spider taunted.

Wake up, wake up, Darlin' Corey
Tell me, how can you sleep so sound?
Dig a grave, dig a grave in the meadow.
Dig a grave in the cold hard ground.
Dig a grave, dig a grave in the meadow.
Gonna lay Darlin' Corey down.

———■◆◄———

Later that night, still sleepless, Valero opened the trap door of the loft and descended into Ryder's workshop. There were two completed coffins atop sawhorses. Both held corpses. No additional coffins were under construction.

Sophia lay curled on the ground between the pine boxes, guarding the work of her master. With a whisper, Valero woke the dog.

She looked up with lids heavy, face groggy. Her mouth opened in an extended yawn.

"Come here," Valero said.

With reluctance, Sophia obeyed. Upon standing, she stretched her front legs. Valero reached down and picked her up. After carrying her outside to the front awning of the workshop, he sat in the middle of the rolling fog. Sophia fell asleep as Valero scratched her ears and stroked her back.

He watched the darkness and listened to the river.

The Spider did not return, nor did her voice. She remained in the loft.

SPENCE Hickman worked like an Indian scout, testing the ground before waving forward Corbin and Felix. Spence possessed surprising grace in the darkness and fog. Felix watched with admiration. The way he moved along the decomposed fence, conscious of each footfall, made Felix wonder about the man's military background. He wondered what he did in the Navy. The presence of Spence had always made him uneasy. His unwillingness to share his past intensified the feeling. He was a man capable of great cruelty, and he had a less predictable nature than Corbin. Spence had two moods: apathy and rage.

Corbin broke the spell of the scene.

"Let's move," he said.

From his horse, which he'd left tied in the woods, Corbin carried a satchel of ammunition. In addition to his rifle, he had two revolvers and a large Bowie knife. Ahead, Spence was armed in similar fashion. Felix carried two guns, his father's revolver and a Smith and Wesson that Corbin supplied.

Spence reached the back wall of the monastery. He waved subtly—a flick of the wrist. Moonlight glinted on a pistol at his waist. Fog stretched around the base of the structure, falling like a blanket over the gardens.

Felix followed Corbin, wary about the noises he made. The leaves beneath his boots were loud. He reminded himself that the men in the front garden were loud, raucous with their laughter and drunkenness. Even at this distance he heard them. Without success, Felix tried to catch the voice of Bennie Wolf. The promise of killing Wolf quickened his heart.

The ruins loomed ahead, a sagging hulk at the apex of the slope. Tall ponderosa pines reached above it at one side. Otherwise, the ruins—like broken teeth where stone crumbled—dominated the sky. There were two entrances along the back wall, one towards the center and one at the far right. Both were open, dark cavities.

When Felix and Corbin reached Spence, the three stood like poised bandits in the monastery's shadow. The fog undulated at their heels. The mist chilled, and for the first time that night Felix was cold. He adjusted his coat. He touched the guns for reassurance. Through the stone, Felix heard the men of Bone-of-Wellington. They argued. He caught the arrogant tones of Alf Parker, Tom's grandfather. For a brief second, Felix thought about Tom.

It would be a shame if he's here. If so, he made his choice.

Spence stood at the threshold of the far right entrance. The frame of the doorway still held trimming, but the door was gone. The debris of rotten wood covered the floor and spilled outside.

Felix recalled gaping holes in the floor of the second story. These were sections of the collapsed ceiling, now rodent havens. Clacking nails and curious squeaks came from within. He nearly smiled at the thought of his scarecrow with a rat's ass poking from its throat, but Spence's dour look kept Felix sober.

Corbin, standing beside Spence, whispered, "Get us to the stairs." He nudged Felix. "We need to get up on the second floor. We'll get us a good fuckin' window from there."

Felix nodded. He was about to reply when a noise, disconnected from the voices out front, made him rigid.

Boots mashed weed stalks.

With a practiced air, Spence slid through the doorway and into the darkness. Corbin stepped gingerly into the debris, and then he gestured for Felix to follow. The men did not make ready their guns. With patience, and without the terror Felix suffered, they stood in silence. Corbin gestured Felix farther inside.

Carefully, Felix navigated the boards.

"Watch the fuckin' rats," Corbin whispered. "Don't make 'em squeal."

Spence leaned for a peek outside. Satisfied, he drew back quietly.

"Hector Bray," he said. "The sheriff."

"He heard us?"

Spence shook his head.

"Taking a piss."

After a breathless moment, Spence looked again.

"Damn," he said.

For the first time, he slid a pistol from his waistband. He propped his rifle against the wall.

"He's lingering."

Felix's heart was in his throat.

Hector paced, drawing closer to the doorway with each return. The grass swished.

Corbin and Spence nodded at one another. Spence raised the gun.

Finally, muttering to himself, Hector moved around the side of the building and back towards the front garden.

Spence lowered the pistol.

Again, Corbin nodded.

Felix released a shuddering breath.

"I'd like to split that bastard's skull," Spence said. "Smug little prick."

Corbin grinned. "But he was so polite to you." He elbowed Felix. "How'd the fucker put it when he caught you drunk? What he say again?"

Spence ignored the chiding. "Far as I'm concerned, he dies first. That'll free up that pretty wife of his."

"I second that," Corbin said. "We'll fuckin' split her in two. Me, I hold no grudges. I guess you want a crack at the Wolf clan?" he whispered to Felix.

Felix considered, and then he said, "Yeah, Bennie."

"He's all yours, kid. Come on now, before that shit-head has to piss again. Get us upstairs."

Felix, feeling useful for the first time that night, led the men through the storage room and into the chapel. This was the first room he recognized. From here he understood how to reach the stairwell. Down the aisle and through the pews, the mustiness of the high-ceilinged room mingling with wood smoke that crept in through the windows, Felix led Corbin and Spence to the doorway. From here, perched at the entrance of the front hall, the solarium and the campfire beyond were visible. The men made silhouettes in the glow of the fire. They'd yet to find the scarecrow. Their laughter and voices grew louder. Someone threw a handful of sticks on the fire and then prodded the flames until they surged. At its zenith, the fire lit a few faces. Felix recognized the plump features of Frank Wolf.

Felix nodded at the stairwell to the left. There was some distance to cover. Once again, Spence took the lead. Crouching lower than the front windows and pausing at each doorway along the length of the solarium, the three shuffled across the stone floor.

The thrill of it, Felix thought, was too much to bear. Despite the damp chill in the air, he sweated profusely.

The window had a history. The original window had been blocked up with bricks. Then someone smashed out the bricks to reopen the window, and then a wood frame was placed in the hole to shore it. The misshapen hole had been hacked open. There was nothing aesthetically pleasing about it. It was crude, bludgeoned.

Moonlight flushed the cell, and a touch of mist covered the floor at the base of the window. Three men stood in the soft light looking outward.

Beyond the front wall, two coyotes, scavenging in the fog, let forth with pathetic yelps, sounds that fell somewhere between a howl and a bark. The treetops were cast with a hint of silver. Smoke from the campfire trailed upward, carrying particles of ash that burned orange and then cooled black. On the other side of the wall, the tethered horses were visible.

Spence and Corbin agreed this was the proper spot. Spence warned Felix not to stand in front of the window, not to speak above a whisper, and to follow their lead without hesitation. Spence pushed him into a corner of the room. Felix stood with a gun in his hand, posed awkwardly in a space teeming with rats.

Corbin went to his knees on the sagging floor. He made certain each weapon was loaded. He pulled free a machete, a blade with a few spots of rust. Holding this, he smiled at Felix.

"I'll try to shoot Bennie's legs out," Corbin whispered. "You can have the pleasure of fuckin' him with this." He placed the blade on the floor.

The kindness restored Felix. He returned the smile.

"I'm not good with a gun," he admitted.

"Just aim it and fire," Spence said. "We'll get the bulk of 'em with these rifles. I got the gate. They won't get out."

"Might get lucky," Corbin said. "You'll find it damn rewardin' if you strike a head."

"Yeah." Spence chuckled.

"Like a fuckin' splash," Corbin said. His eyes were alight, his energy contagious.

Felix grew aroused.

"Looks like throwin' rocks into a pond." Corbin gestured, moving his hands in the arc of a splash, a gesture made visible by the ample moonlight. "You'll love it. Hell, I can't get enough of it. Anytime I look out a window I think it. I see somebody walk by and I imagine how the fuckin' splash would come out."

"You hit the face low, though," Spence said, "there ain't much splash. Looks like kickin' in a melon. Just caves. Comes off in a few big chunks sometimes."

"Big enough gun," Corbin agreed. "Sometimes it'll spray the teeth."

"That's true," Spence conceded. He chuckled again. "Like pumpkin seeds."

"Alright, fuckers," Corbin said. "Let's get it."

He stood and cocked the Winchester. The noise reverberated through the upper corridor.

Felix grimaced. His palms sweated, so he wiped his hands on his coat in preparation. He gripped the oak stock of the revolver, and he pulled back the hammer.

"Sheriff's out there," Spence said. "I count twelve. Take a look."

Corbin peered out.

Felix crept from his corner and did the same.

"There's Bray propped against the wall. Fucker looks like he's sleepin'. That's my first shot. Then I move steadily towards the gate away from the fire. Corbin, you light 'em up right at the fire. Kid, you do your damned best to shoot at them and not hit yourself, this wall, or one of us."

"I got it," Felix said.

His chest was so tight he barely breathed. The tang of copper rose on the back of his tongue. It was the same feeling he experienced the night before, poised above the sleeping form of his father with a hammer in his hand. It was a wonderful and exhilarating feeling.

Spence placed the rifle against his shoulder.

"Pick your target and make this one count," he said. "Get that Parker kid. He'll be the quickest. Put one right in his belly."

"Shit, he just hopped off the wall. Fuck's sake." Corbin turned to Felix. "Kid, where'd you put your fuckin' scarecrow?"

Felix scanned the shadowed corner of the garden.

"Right where they're looking," he said. He grinned.

"Pile up, boys," Spence said. "That's it. Good work, kid."

DEAR GOD, *don't tell me you believe that yarn. Ryder will tell you it's true. When we get back, ask him.*

He'd know. The way I understand it, Old Man Argo was a lieutenant in his unit.

Pierce Ryder's full of shit. If you ain't learned that yet I don't know what to tell you. You don't really believe it, do you? Shit, you do.

I ain't discounting it.

Jesus Christ.

Dumb sonnuva bitch.

How you know it ain't there?

'Cause it ain't likely. What use would there be in it?

Less likely to be stolen. Got the train to get it in and out. If I had a bunch of silver to hide, I don't think this would be a bad place to hide it.

Old Man Argo was a lieutenant? I thought he was colonel or somethin'.

It's accordin' to what mood Ryder's in when he tells the story. Sometimes he's the president of the fuckin' United States. Fuckin' Argo.

I'm telling you, it's a goddamned yarn. Only a fool would believe it.

Count me a fool then.

I already do. It's a story kids believe. Tom, Bennie, you all hear that story growin' up?

I heard it.

Yes, sir.

You believe it?

Hector drifted closer to sleep, conversation from around the fire reaching him opaquely. The men argued about whether Old Man Argo buried a cache of silver in Bone-of-Wellington. It was an old wives' tale, but Hector offered no opinion on the matter.

Obnoxiously, Frank Wolf was adamant the silver didn't exist, and Hector wasn't interested in backing up the man's judgment. He wanted to sleep. The quicker he fell asleep the quicker morning would arrive. He experienced a sensation on his wrist, and he looked down to find a tick attached to his skin.

Damned ticks, he thought.

There was no telling where they'd gotten to under his clothes. He pinched off several during the evening, but if ticks were his largest problem, then so be it. He could live with that.

Hector thought of his home and the warm body of Constance waiting in their bed. As Hector closed his eyes again, Tom Parker called out from the wall.

"Hey, pap."

Men around the fire looked up. Hector craned his neck.

"Hey, pap, there's somethin' in the grass over there."

Alf Parker stood from his spot by the fire. "What is it?"

Everybody fell quiet, watching Tom.

Chasing ghosts, Hector thought.

He rested his head against stone. The men were wrong earlier about a creeper in the grass. Hector, per their request, had made a circuit around the building, and he found nothing. This was more of the same. They'd see shapes and hear stalkers all night.

Tom hopped off the wall, landing with a jarring thud in the dirt.

"Looks like a man," he said, cautiously now. His voice slowed. "Looks like somebody sleepin' in the grass. Over against the wall."

Frank Wolf bellowed, "Alf, your boy's losin' his goddamn mind."

Alf gave Frank the usual sentiment, but the men stood and walked toward the area where Tom pointed, regardless. Reluctantly, Hector looked, too. As he stared, a shape manifested in the darkness.

Hector went cold.

The men crowded around Tom.

Hector stood.

"Wake him up, Tommy," Frank said. "Give him a drink."

Tom moved towards a shield of briars in one of the garden's corners. He stopped close to the shape.

"You gotta be fuckin' with me," Tom said. "Pap, come have a look at this."

"Goddamn it," Alf said. "Stop that. What is it?"

"It's a corpse," Tom said. "There's flies on him."

"You sure that ain't a deer carcass?" someone asked.

In a surreal voice, Tom added, "He's wearin' clothes." He paused. "Got his head blown clean off." He moved briars aside.

The men drew closer, tightening a circle around Tom.

Hector pushed through. He heard the flies.

How had they missed such a thing? What else did they miss?

When Hector was at Tom's side, the corpse came fully into view. A spade of orange firelight reached its neck, while the rest waited in shadow and moonlight. Whoever it was, he'd been dead for some time. He was rotten, but the worst of the scent had been siphoned off.

"What in God's name?" Frank said. His tone sobered.

Tom looked at him. "There's a goddamn rat buried in his throat." He let the briars fall.

"Like he's been posed," Hector said.

He looked back at the gate. No one stood near it. Everyone was packed into the corner—all twelve packed tight.

He drew us into a killing box, Hector thought, and it was a rapid, blistering idea that was very real. There was nothing paranoid about it. *This is what he wanted all along.*

"He's still here," Hector said, shocked by the revelation, by his stupidity.

"What?"

Before Hector responded, the first shots rang across the woods, near enough to sound like explosions.

Two shots, followed by a lagging third shot, threw the camp into a frenzy.

A bullet struck Hector's side like someone swinging a hammer against his ribs. In an instant he was delirious with pain, shocked by the outburst of gunfire and the whirl of men running towards the front gate.

Once the rifle blasts began, the shooting didn't stop. For several minutes, one shot followed another. No one had the mind to draw a weapon and return fire. It all happened too quickly. The heroics of such a thing would have done no good. The posse showed itself to be manhunters in name alone.

As Hector fell onto his side and writhed, the agony of shattered ribs going to his brain, he scanned the darkness for a sign of gunmen. There was too much shooting to be Felix alone. Beyond the firelight all was black. While the men fell around him, Hector struggled to his knees, cradling the wound at this side, feeling nausea at the blood running over his arm. He crawled toward the gate.

Please, Jesus, Hector thought, praying. *Please not now. Please don't widow Constance.*

Pride. All this because of pride.

Jesus, please.

Ahead, Alf Parker fell hard against the earth, a shot slammed into his back. Hector crawled closer. To his horror, another bullet caught the old man's skull, which was already planted in the ground, opening his brain and spraying blood.

Terror moved Hector. His mind went numb in protection. He heard no shots, although men continued to fall, bodies writhed, and bullets kicked up dirt and blasted stone. One of the bullets struck Hector's foot, tearing open his boot, shattering bones, but he only sensed the pressure of it. Another bullet nearly ruined his hand, obliterating the fingernail on his index finger.

Heedlessly, he clawed at the earth and dragged himself. The ground turned muddy with blood. Hector didn't feel the slop. It occurred to him that his mind had him moving, but his body sank into the mud. Alf was behind him now. He looked over his shoulder. No one remained standing. Someone (Tom Parker?) had fallen face first into the fire, and the flames burned at his ear and engulfed his hair. His skin peeled back like snake rind, blackening. The pain did not move him, so he was already dead.

Ahead, Bennie Wolf crawled to the gate. He was the closest to making it to the horses. Three gaping wounds on his thighs hung open like ribbons. Another shot tore his hand, ripping away fingers like so much debris. Bennie fell onto his side, crying out.

Hector willed himself to move, to keep going, but his body refused. Finally, he collapsed on his stomach.

He didn't hear the shooting stop, and he didn't witness the shocked stillness of the forest that followed.

ONE MONTH PRIOR: AN INTERLUDE

About fifty yards behind Rand's Hotel stood a crude platform and awning that edged the railroad tracks. Men called it the depot, although there were no tickets to be bought and sold. Twice a month a locomotive that began its trek in Omaha crossed the river and pulled into town, hissing steam and burping smoke. The loading bay at the sawmill was the train's first stop in Bone-of-Wellington.

Then, laden with timber, the locomotive eased into the depot. The train was not built for passengers (its purpose was to truck wood and coal), but Old Man Argo had arranged for the special privilege of travelers. He had enough money to change the course of things when it suited his needs. For a fee, the train escorted folks from Bone-of-Wellington southward, dropping them at the next town on the line, Trinity Hill, which was a journey of sixty miles. Trinity Hill was a growing town with a real depot, and from there one could hitch a passenger locomotive to San Francisco or back east towards the Mississippi.

It was at the Bone-of-Wellington depot, however, that Corbin Blum, standing tall beneath the awning, his back against a post, convinced Felix. Spence was taking a final drink at Rand's before joining them, so the two were alone. The locomotive was at the mill, loading. The railroad men were drinking beers. Corbin and Felix stood together on the platform. There had always been tension between them, one that Felix found new and odd. Corbin wanted something.

The perfume of a mutilated cow, butchered for the menu at Rand's, hung in the air. There was a cistern in the back lot where the blood drained into an underground branch of the river.

Corbin had worked at the mill two months, and in that time he came to know Felix rather well. He knew what the boy wanted out of life, and he knew the urges the boy harbored. For the past week, ever since he admitted that he and Spence were heading on to Trinity Hill, Corbin encouraged Felix to talk about those urges. He told the boy some lurid tales. The forbidden things he revealed shocked Felix's senses, but they also thrilled him. Corbin even told of the prison riot in Arkansas that hardened his heart.

It was this candidness that won the kid's trust.

Corbin told Felix how much he was needed. He made promises.

"All those books you read," he said, "you can do anything you want. You do this and you'll be able to do anything. Anything." He nodded at the hulking sawmill. "You won't never have to work in a hellhole like that again."

"What do you want me to do?" It was a necessary question, although Felix knew the answer. He wanted to hear Corbin say it, not hint at it. Felix needed the courage.

"What you already wanna do. It'll do you a helluva lotta good beyond the money. Believe me on that. There ain't anything like gettin' that feelin' off your chest."

"Just my old man?"

Corbin looked up the railroad tracks. He watched a crow soar low and grip the track with its talons. It was a large bird, black with the sheen of oil.

"Your old man would be enough," he said finally. "Whatever it takes to raise the hue and cry. They'll put their best men in the posse. They're that way. Then we'll be waitin' on 'em. With those men gone we'll split the town wide."

"What if I get caught?"

Corbin admired the crow. It hopped along the rail without grace. Then, unsatisfied, the bird beat its wings and was airborne again. It landed in a tree occupied by another crow, this one shorter and stockier. They tolerated one an-

other's presence on the branch. The sight reminded Felix of Corbin and Spence.

"Don't get caught," Corbin said. "They'll skin you like a fuckin' deer and hang your bag from that water tank." He laughed at the image. "There's nothin' I can do if you get caught."

With gravity, Felix nodded. Out of the corner of his eye, he saw Spence approach. Hickman carried two saddlebags over his wide shoulders. He kept a somber pace and kept his eyes to the ground, absorbed in thought.

"You're sure there's silver?" Felix asked.

With the probe of his good eye, Corbin stared through him. Challenged, all personality drained from his features. It was the effect of a man poised to faint, but instead of blood draining and leaving his features pallid, a shadow passed over him, and what was drained was humanity.

"What do you fuckin' think we've been doin' the last two months?"

Spence, dropping his saddlebags on the platform, broke the tension.

"Engineer's gettin' ready to head back up to the mill," he said. He cracked his neck. "Won't be long."

WITH great effort, Hector opened heavy eyes. He had blacked out from pain and loss of blood, but for how long he didn't know.

He didn't renew his effort to crawl, however, because three men stood near him, surveying the carnage. Two of the men walked along, prodding bodies with rifles. The other stood near Bennie Wolf, and he gripped a machete. Bennie was alive. He was saying something to the man above him.

Hector remained still. Soon came his turn. The rifle came down hard against his broken ribs, and the pain was like a white light behind his eyes, an explosion in his skull. He did not move, and he did not breathe. The man with a rifle moved on, satisfied. Hector's brain was too addled to think clearly, but he thought he recognized the man with a machete. Creasing his eyes, he peered through matted eyelashes.

While the other men looked on and chuckled, the man with a blade hacked at Bennie with fury. He cleaved into the skull so deeply that he struggled to free the blade. Bennie moaned weakly. He didn't shout or fight back. The man with the machete worked on Bennie's neck. He was severing the boy's head. Finally, he knelt and used the machete like a saw, pressing down with a hand on each end to break the gristle.

With certainty, Hector saw that Felix Hines wielded the blade.

"Harder than it looks, ain't it?" one of the men said.

"Spence, you remember that prison guard? That one you tried with a coffee can lid?"

The other man laughed.

Spence?

Bleeding profusely, praying for strength, Hector fainted away.

The monastery resembled a battlefield. To the world, he was a dead man, prostrate in a garden of corpses.

Felix kicked at the head, and he cleaved until it broke loose. Bennie Wolf's eyes looked like withered apples sunk into his skull. His mouth was agape, which was fitting. Felix was silent, transfixed by the sight. The only sign he felt anything at all was a tremble in his hand, the one that gripped the blade.

The other men, tiring of his game, moved to the front gate and smoked cigarettes. Quietly, they talked of plans. Occasionally they turned and surveyed the garden, sensitive to any movement.

Hector, embedded in the mud, slept.

Deep in the woods beyond the gate, the scavenging coyotes fled in terror, as did the birds and deer. Animals twisted through the pine groves, away from the monastery, down the hillside.

Even as they fled, the coyotes, and the crows above them, noted the tang of blood in the air.

WITH a pick and shovel braced on his shoulder, Valero garnered looks. The faces, all strangers to him, didn't turn away in shyness or decency. As they stared, the people talked in hushed tones. On the front deck of a lopsided and boorish emporium, three women, one elderly and none matching the elegance of Constance Bray, snickered.

This, one said, was a vagabond in search of a train.

In a fogged alleyway, Valero passed two brutish types on their way to the mill. The men watched him pass. One of the men noted the gun that nearly fell from Valero's coat pocket. He felt the suspicion of their gazes, which was not a surprise with the recent killings. He made no attempt to respond or protect himself. He walked on.

Unkempt and unshaven, smelling of wood smoke, beer, and animal decay, the stray dog Valero kept his hat low and his face dark. To look at him, one would imagine he was deep in thought. Such was the stillness of his downcast face. However, Valero had no thoughts worth divulging that morning. He was numb and filthy, and he only moved because he had a desire to earn breakfast. Any other thought he had was mundane. When the chemical stench of the river came to him, for instance, he thought about wading into its current with his clothes on. His trousers and shirt had hardened over the last few months. His coat was a tent in sore need of airing.

As he started up the trail to the graveyard, the tools on his shoulder clanked and knocked.

A child, fiddling with a network of chains behind one of the shacks, observed, "It's only a gravedigger."

Peering back, Valero noticed that the boy comforted a younger sibling, also toying with a knot, who took umbrage at a stranger in their midst.

The cemetery stood at the edge of a mound, only slightly higher than the shacks below. A wooden fence, thrown together in haste, wrapped the contour. The entrance was a frame of wooden boards, spaced wide enough for a wagon to pull through and high enough for a tall man to pass through without ducking his head. The cemetery was nameless, offering no comfort to the bereaved. Valero wondered if harboring the body of a murdered child would change that fact.

He walked through the entrance, resting the pick against the fence as he passed. Ryder had placed two stones on the ground where the larger graves were to be. The stones were placed on either side of the daughter, with the father on the left and mother on the right. Bryson, Willa, and Cora Hines. When their crosses were erected and their flat stones placed, all would read the same date. The graves would be here long after men abandoned Bone-of-Wellington. The crosses would fall, and the fence would fall, but the graves would remain beneath the earth.

Waiting for what? Valero wondered.

His mother, before she was too ill, read him snippets of the Bible. When he was old enough, she made him read passages aloud in her presence. It was how she taught him to read. Unlike Ryder, she didn't value other books. Valero came to know the stories well.

His father was not a religious man. He never had time for lofty thoughts. His life and concerns were here on the ground, he said. There was nothing above, and there was nothing below. Valero's mother thought his father a simpleton for this.

He planted the shovel and removed the earth. The grave opened.

Believing was the more difficult path. On that point his mother was correct. Life inclined Valero to believe in the vein of his father, that there was nothing above, and that nothing followed life. That these people were victims of an enraged animal was the easiest thing in the world to believe. It took no leap of faith, no faith at all, only observation. But it was a distant and cold way to see things, and Valero couldn't see it so simply. He had more of his mother in him than he cared to admit. He differed with her on a key point, however. Where she would say that Jesus harbored and welcomed these folks, that they were lucky to have passed, he would say something more malignant had occurred. The world was hostile. The whole universe was malignant, and if it targeted you… well, there was no loving god waiting when it caught you.

Whatever waited on the Hines family hated rather than loved.

Furiously, Valero stomped the shovel deeper. The pile of earth grew at his side.

He wondered if his mother found this out in the end. He wondered if the thought occurred to her as the rope tightened, or when she looked up at the horse and Hangman, or when rocks ripped the flesh of her stomach. Or, he thought, stomping the shovel, when her son stood and watched, a gun in his hand, and did nothing. He wondered if she thought God loved man then.

God took pleasure in such things. If not, then why?

Valero stopped, his chest heaving from exertion, and he gathered his breath. He looked down at Willa's grave. Any god with power was a god of animals, and he was a brutal god. Leaning on the shovel, he turned his gaze to the river. Birds swooped at the muddy current, cutting through the morning mist that hung above the water.

There was a god of the living, Valero was convinced, the malignant and cruel force of the world. He was the Hangman. And there was a god of the dead, a god of the hanged as he liked to think of her. She was the Spider.

Yet you chase her off. Why? She tries to protect you. You run away. She came to you last night, and you tore at her web. You turned your back. Now she's silent.

I killed that old man, Valero thought. *He did nothing. He was miserable.*

You killed him. You pretend to know he was innocent. How could you know? By appearance?

As your mother's Bible says, The heart is deceitful above all things, and desperately wicked: who can know it? *How could you know what was in his heart? You couldn't know, but she knew. She warned you because she knew.*

She lies.

What need would she have for lies?

"Elijah!"

Valero turned to see Ryder walking slump-shouldered into the cemetery. He was not an early riser. There was no sign he was awake when Valero left that morning, and his face was heavy with want of sleep. Valero was perturbed at the old man for dashing his train of thought.

Then, in the pit of his mind, he wondered if Ryder knew his thoughts and chased them away on purpose. Guardedly, he stood behind the shovel, watching the man's eyes for a hint of betrayal.

"Son, I got the gruel warming out back of the shed. Why don't you get your belly full before wearin' yourself out again?"

Valero shook his head, but he said nothing.

"Why the hell you lookin' at me like that?"

Valero looked at the ground. He found his coat. He located the revolver in the pocket.

"I like to work before I eat," he said.

Through the gates, yipping in protest, came Sophia. Her tail wagged, and her tongue hung at the side of her mouth. Unlike Ryder, she was alert and awake. Valero knelt when she came to him. He scratched her ear.

"She stay with you all night?" Ryder asked. "She usually sleeps in my bed."

Valero nodded.

"I'll be damned," Ryder said. "That's one thing she's never done. She must fancy you."

Valero said nothing.

"Come down and eat when you see fit," Ryder said. "I'll be up in a bit with the other shovel. You're a bundle of joy this morning, chum. Jesus." He turned to go. "Come on, Sophia."

The dog sat on her haunches and clamped her mouth, resolute.

"To hell with both of you then," Ryder said. "Maybe it's me."

As he walked away, Valero returned to digging. Sophia watched, stretching out and pressing her stomach against the damp grass. Valero tried to regain his thoughts, but his mind was blank, numbed. He felt like Sophia watched over him, but when he checked he found her panting with her eyes closed.

"That's a good gal," he whispered.

Despite the blackness of his mood, Valero smiled.

THE garden was alive with the din of flies. The thrumming spread over the monastery grounds, a chord of music, and it reached into the trees. There were thousands of flies, some darting in the air, others frantic on the stiffening flesh. Their monotony could lull one into sleep.

Sunlight, strong since daybreak, flushed the garden, filled the solarium, and blistered the remains lying motionless in the weeds and mud. The stench of excrement and offal filled the air like a stockyard under the burn of August.

The garden, Spence commented, smelled like Chicago.

Felix found Corbin in the high-ceilinged chapel, sitting alone at the altar, a priest with no audience in the pews. His picture was one of symmetry, sitting as he did between the rows. He sat with his legs crossed, his back slumped, and he ate from a slab of jerky. He stripped each piece with the grain of the meat, thin filaments that he dangled over his mouth like worms, released, and then chewed methodically. Corbin was so skeletal it surprised Felix to see him eating. He always assumed Corbin smoked cigarettes for his meals. The man weighed no more than a woman. He was like a stage ghost, a waif of dirty gauze.

Felix moved down the aisle, footfalls echoing in the cavernous room. He wondered what a man like Corbin would do with a wealth of silver. Unlike Spence, who'd take the money to San Francisco and blow it as fast as it would burn, he figured Corbin would use the money to disappear. He'd buy a place in the wilderness. Felix had never been a good judge of character, though, so he wanted to ask.

His grim demeanor accentuated by several days' growth of scraggly beard, Corbin looked up from his meal. His good eye found Felix, while the shrunken eye ticked and wandered, dead as the men in the garden. When he spoke, although soft, his voice reverberated in the chamber.

"Where's Spence?" Corbin asked.

Felix sat on the front pew.

"Last I saw he was taking care of the horses."

Corbin nodded. He stripped another thread of jerky. Reclining his head, he dropped the strand between his lips. His Adam's apple bobbed as he swallowed.

"Did he have the wagon?"

He had, but Felix didn't know from where the wagon had come.

Sensing his confusion, Corbin said, "We brought it along. It's our'n."

"For what?"

To this, Corbin didn't reply.

The silver, Felix realized.

As Corbin finished the jerky, silence passed. There was dried blood on Corbin's hands. He'd scrubbed his own hands clean with tufts of grass pilfered from the back fields. Corbin didn't mind having blood on his food. To him it was only so much dirt.

High above, creepers snaked inside the chapel, covering the wooden frame of the windows and casting shadows in the sunlight. The shadow of vines crossed Felix's lap.

Flies in the garden were audible, even here.

Feeling intimidated, Felix said, as if to a friend, "You seem unhappy."

Corbin shook his head.

It occurred to Felix that this was the man's last gamble. He was making one last effort at life. If there were no silver, Corbin would blow out his brains. He looked like he was in the mood to do so, as if doubt gnawed at him. It was not a subject to broach. It had to be unspoken.

"Always a fuckin' crash after somethin' like last night," Corbin said. He laughed. Reaching into his ragged vest, he pulled out a pouch of tobacco. Patiently, he rolled a cigarette.

Patiently, Felix waited.

Corbin lit the cigarette and took a draw. The smoke roiled from his nose in twin streams, obscuring his face.

"Feels like when you need a smoke," he said. "You smoke?"

Felix shook his head.

"How'd it feel?" Corbin asked.

He slipped from the altar. His boots slapped against the stone floor. He walked across the aisle and, tucking the cigarette between his lips, joined Felix on the pew. He sat so close that Felix felt his warmth and smelled him.

"Which one?" Felix asked.

"Oh, not last night. That didn't mean anything. I meant your old man."

Felix didn't understand why, but he nearly cried. It was with a swell of emotion, with a release, that he said, "It was the best moment of my entire life. You ever read *The Odyssey*?"

Corbin inhaled deeply. Upon release, he said, "You know I can't read anything that has more than four fuckin' letters in it. I ain't smart like you."

"Well, never mind then. It felt like it was supposed to happen."

"What about Bennie Wolf?"

"That was just something I wanted to do. It felt good."

Corbin laughed.

"What'd you do with his fuckin' head?"

Felix reddened.

"I saw you take it off and set it in the woods. You plan on keepin' it?"

"I thought about it."

"You sure you don't smoke? You oughta start. Good for the nerves."

Felix took the cigarette. The tip was wet with Corbin's spit. He placed it in his mouth, and there was something sensual about sharing it. The smoke was harsh against his throat. He didn't inhale much, and then he coughed out the rest. The closeness of Corbin made him nervous. Felix returned the cigarette, touching Corbin's bony hand as he did so.

"Tell me about when you used to follow the gallows," Felix said. "Did you know Spence then?"

"No," Corbin said. "Me and Spence didn't meet until we was in Arkansas. We worked on a fuckin' chain gang." He laughed. "Spence hadn't been outta the Navy long. No, it was a long time before that. I was your age. Why you like this story so much?"

"I want to do it," Felix admitted.

"There were two or three of us, dependin' on when and where. You know they call an opium eater a fiend? We called ourselves fiends, too, 'cause it was like that. We got addicted to it. I was in a fuckin' town called Marmet, and there was gonna be a hangin'. Some bastard. He stole a fuckin' pig or somethin' stupid. In Marmet that was a hangin' offense. They advertised the fuckin' thing. I ain't kiddin'. They printed up a poster and fastened it to the window of the telegraph office. Said somethin' like 'Come see Big Bill Cochise,' whatever the hell his name was. 'Today he bites the dust.' And they was fuckin' serious. So I went. They had food and stuff. Kids. Games. Music. They marched Cochise out, made him split the crowd. All the while, they was pummelin' the guy. Just beatin' the fuckin' piss outta him. His face was all puffy, bruised, nose red as a beetroot.

"Watchin' him get strung up gave me the biggest fuckin' sting of pleasure of my life. When that rope pulled taut and his neck snapped like a fuckin' cord—I couldn't stand it. His bones popped." Corbin clicked his tongue in imitation of the sound. "I got so excited I had to buy a woman that night. I could've drained my balls then and there. I couldn't even hide my whore pipe. Anyway, that hangman cut up the rope and sold it. I bought a piece for a nickel."

"You still have it?"

"Nah. When I went to Arkansas, they took everything I owned and threw it in an incinerator for meanness. That was my start. I traveled around for a year, watchin' bastards hang."

"I want to do that," Felix said.

"Best thing about it was I wasn't alone. I started to see faces I knew in the crowds and afterwards in the saloons. There's a whole bunch of fuckin' people that follow the gallows, kid. I made friends with a few. We traveled together and looked out for each other. Called ourselves 'gallows fiends'."

"What made you dig one up?" Felix asked. He knew the stories, but he loved the way Corbin told them. He loved the tension in the man's voice.

"Oh hell, you know how it is. You gotta fuckin' outdo yourself. That's a whole other thrill, though." Corbin paused, watching Felix. "You remind me a lot of me at that age. Although I wasn't no brain like you. You know, Spence is sharp, too. Bet you wouldn't have guessed that. He did a lot of stuff when he was with the Confederate Navy. Secret stuff, by the way he tells it, with fuckin' codes and shit."

Shyly, Felix looked at the floor.

"Know what else I tried at your age?"

"What's that?"

Corbin mashed the cigarette stub on the pew.

"Be better if I showed you. Then you can try one on me."

Felix looked up.

Corbin moved closer, until the heat of his rancid breath touched Felix's face.

"Gotta relax," Corbin said. "Can you do that for your old buddy?"

"I'm relaxed," Felix said, although he was anything but.

"Let's see how fuckin' hard that talk got you. I bet you're all wet and lathered." Reaching into Felix's lap, Corbin rubbed his palm along the erection that strained his pants. He leaned over, bending at the waist. "I'm gonna take it out." He looked up with his good eye. "How 'bout you be my friend?" he asked. "I've wanted to do this a while."

Felix nodded. His breathing was short and quick.

As Corbin got his hand in Felix's waistband, a thump at the back of the chapel made another presence known. Corbin withdrew his hand and straightened. Felix, burning red, turned to see Spence standing in the doorway. He rapped on the wall with his fist. How long Spence had listened, Felix could not say, but he was humiliated by the idea.

Felix tried to run through what just happened. It was too much. The excitement made him lightheaded.

"What are you girls yappin' about?" Spence asked.

He wasn't angry. Rather, he was amused. He had a thick cigar in his mouth, burned halfway to the hilt.

Corbin stood from the pew. He wasn't flustered, but his demeanor changed.

"Your ears burnin'? Hey, where the hell'd you get that thing?"

Spence pulled the cigar from his mouth and clenched it between his fingers. He looked at it in admiration.

"Old man out there had it in his shirt pocket. He'd only smoked a third of it. It's good leaf."

Felix stood. His erection had died, leaving a wet spot against his trousers. His heart remained fast.

"Let's get that wagon loaded," Spence said. "We gotta big night ahead of us."

With that, he turned and left the chapel. His footsteps echoed in the corridor. Corbin, who said nothing of what had passed, was close on his heels.

Felix stood alone, his mind reeling. The natural light in the chapel was the shade of pewter, and the room was quiet. He hesitated, feeling confused. Eventually, he followed Corbin towards the chatter of busy flies.

PARKED in the gateway, the wagon jittered with the restlessness of the tethered horses. The animals were spooked. Spence had fastened two stout horses, both of which had belonged to men in the posse, to the four-wheeled flatbed. The wagon was old and meager, edged with short walls. The springs were noisy. The planks were dry rotted, leaving crumbled indentations like scar tissue.

Spence placed the first body, that of Alf Parker, on the boards. The corpse was rigid as stone, the spine twisted in a manner that made the body teeter when the horses fidgeted. The old man weighed no more than a hundred pounds. A portion of his head was missing.

As Spence and Corbin smoked another cigar, Felix wandered through the bodies, parting clouds of flies. The air was moist and hot, hastening putrefaction. Each inhalation in the garden was fetid. Felix knew all these men, but familiarity with their shapes, their faces, their clothes inspired no remorse. He looked upon the men as a lizard looks upon a foreign object.

Tom Parker lay face down in the ashes of a campfire. Felix stopped and paid his respects. He recognized Tom by his boots and pants. There was a gaping hole in Tom's back where a bullet exited. From the look of the wound, a shot pierced his heart before making the hole. Felix wondered if he had fired the shot. It was unlikely. He looked up to the second-story window from which he'd fired, and he doubted he hit anything except the mud. Whoever fired it, the shot felled Parker and dropped him into the flames. The fire, before he extinguished it with his bulk, burned his face, leaving a black mask of char. The scent of incinerated hair clung to him.

It was unfortunate, Felix conceded, remembering how Parker tried to help him fit in at the mill. Tom was decent. Felix never knew him to mean harm.

So long, Tom, he thought.

"You want one of these cigars?" Spence called. "It'll chase off some of the stink."

Felix shook his head.

"I don't mind it," he said quietly. He turned and walked back to Corbin and Spence and their cloud of smoke.

Around the cigar, Corbin said, "We're gonna take some of these bodies into town. It'll stir their fuckin' blood."

Looking around, Felix said, "I suppose it will. What about the rest of the men in town? This is only a few of them."

"We have plans for that tonight," Spence said brusquely. "This is ain't your game of chess. It'll do you well not to think too many moves ahead."

Felix nodded.

"We got it thought out start to finish," Corbin said. His manner was easier than that of Spence. He touched Felix's shoulder.

"You're gonna put some pressure on Pierce Ryder, aren't you?" Felix asked.

"Among others."

"Old Ryder knows where it's hidden, doesn't he?"

Corbin removed his cigar. He winked.

"He just might, kid."

"He knows," Spence said. "Now if you're satisfied, hop to."

One body at a time, they performed the gruesome labor. Spence picked up the bodies and thrust them into the wagon on his own, while Corbin and Felix handled the others together. Most of the bodies were rigid, but a few others were soft. When the soft bodies thudded into the wagon, gas escaped their holes like groans.

Felix stopped, standing over the body of Hector Bray. There was copious blood. He'd taken a bullet in the ribs. He'd taken another bullet in the foot. Torn flesh showed where the boot was open. Flies swarmed his wounds covetously.

When Corbin approached, smacking his hands and puffing the cigar, Felix remarked, "It's like in Homer."

The thought hit him with some potency.

"The sheriff? I thought his name was Hector."

"It's Hector, like in *The Iliad*," Felix said.

Corbin shrugged.

"Like Achilles at Troy. Achilles hooked Hector's corpse to a chariot and dragged him around the walls. Hector's father, the king, and his mother and his wife had to stand and watch."

"Who the hell cares? Pick him up. It's too damn hot out to tarry."

Felix knelt, grabbing Hector by the shoulders. The body was pliant, and the arms dangled as he and Corbin lifted him from the mud. The wagon, laden with flesh, sank with the sheriff's weight.

"Pretty sight, kid" Corbin remarked. Again, he rubbed Felix's shoulder.

Thus shamefully did Achilles in his fury dishonor Hector, Felix thought.

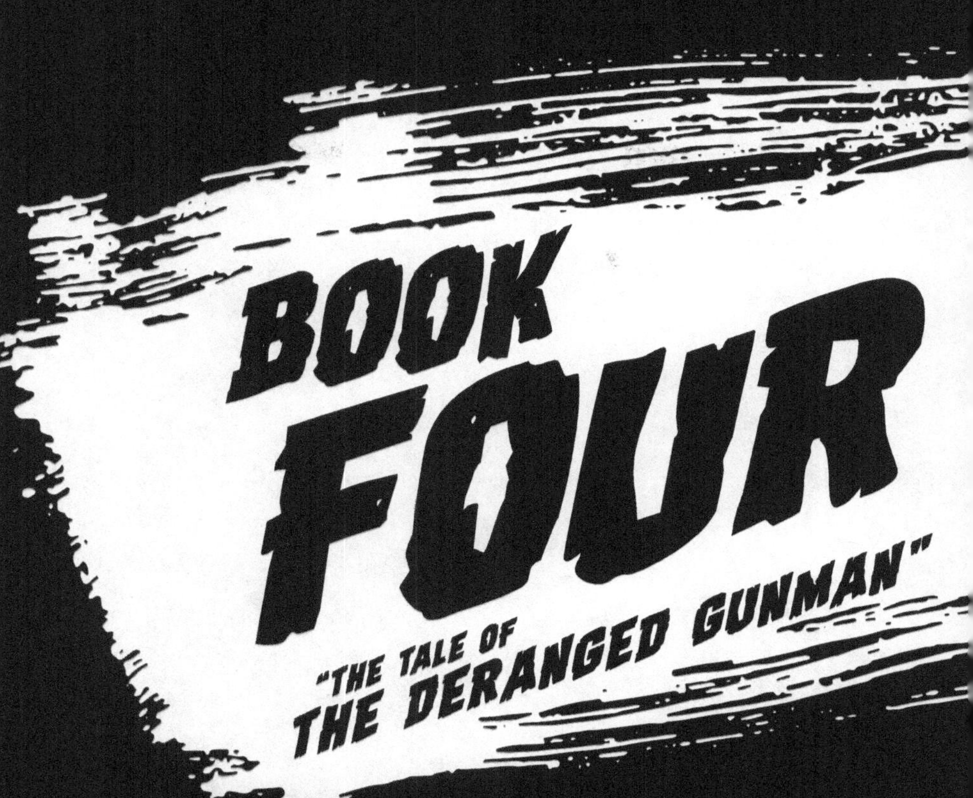

BOOK FOUR
"THE TALE OF THE DERANGED GUNMAN"

BEING AN ACCOUNT OF
HOW BULLETS WANT BLOOD.
BEING, TOO, A RECKONING.

THE livery stable in Bone-of-Wellington was a large barn that stood beside Rand's. Arguably, it was the finest building in the settlement. The boards were straight, tight, and painted a shade of burgundy. Paint gave the stable an air of elegance, contrasting as it did with the bleak and splinter-edged buildings that surrounded it. It was a dab of color in a sea of grey, like a bush of roses in a dead field. Presently, the stable held eleven horses.

Housing an animal was free to anyone who worked at the mill, courtesy of the Argo family. It was a generous perk, although most couldn't afford the luxury of owning a horse. A good robber baron, Old Man Argo had thought of that, because five horses in the stable were available to rent. Four of the five were heavy draft horses, built for toil. The other was a Morgan with a beautiful brown coat and blond tail, built for decoration and riding. Pierce Ryder managed the stable along with his other duties, but the day-to-day drudgery of running the place (feeding, watering, exercising the animals, cleaning the stalls) fell to a kid named Wiley. Wiley's father worked at the mill.

With a quiet mind, Valero walked through the front gate of the livery like a shadow off the bright street. Inside, it was cool and dark. Outside, the perpetual mud of the main thoroughfare hardened into a tapestry of cracked basins. The floor of the livery gave like a plowed field covered in straw. The aroma of manure and horse-flesh was pleasant, almost idyllic.

Valero thought of all the horses he'd owned in his time, and he was heartsick. There were too many, most of them very brief. He had to see Maureen again.

Wiley, sharpening a wicked-looking sickle, placed his whetstone at the side of his chair and stood. With the sickle in his grasp, he'd be adept in a canebrake. He placed the blade on the seat. The sun caught its razor edge. For a child no more than twelve, he was a hard worker. His hands were tough, and his small frame, no more than five feet, was muscled. His face was too care-worn for that of a boy. He took in more hard times than his years should've allowed. He approached Valero like a man his equal.

"Who would you be?" Wiley asked.

Valero looked over the boy's head towards a line of box stalls.

"Callin' on a girl," he said absently. "I'm told she's quartered here."

"None of these horses belong to you. You lookin' to rent?"

"I'm here to call on her, not take her. Her name's Maureen."

"Oh, hellfire, you're the trollop."

Valero stared.

"The guy that brought her in from the woods," Wiley said.

Valero shook his head.

"Find a new word," he said. "Ain't quite what that means."

Wiley's face reddened. "My pa says it."

The kid's insolence tired Valero.

"Where's Maureen?" he asked.

"Second to last stall at the back," the boy said.

Valero touched the brim of his hat. He walked deeper into the shadows, finding the air cooler. After hours of digging a grave in the sun, his blood boiled. His skin was baked. The darkness felt good. He'd filled his stomach with gruel before walking to the stable. Rightly, he questioned a fear that Ryder poisoned the vat of porridge. It was nonsense, Valero reasoned, but he thought about the possibility with each bite.

Maureen leaned over the gate that enclosed her in the stall, observing Valero with a sideways glance. She knew he was here to visit. She looked clean and content, although weary in the eyes. Her roan coat, white hairs mingling with the chestnut brown, was brushed clean, as was her once-tangled mane. Maureen reminded Valero of a woman bathed and ready for bed. She flicked her lips, exposing teeth as he approached.

"How they treatin' you, gal?" Valero said.

It was good to be with her, calming, like a friend. He stroked her broad neck, moving delicately around the scabs. The lash on her snout was healing. Maureen leaned into his touch.

You were dealt a bad hand, he thought, trying to find more personality in her eyes. It was there, below a film of defense. She snorted and shook her hair. Valero reached over the gate. He scooped a handful of oats from her feed bag. The horse ate from his palm, wetting his fingers. Being with the horse made him feel young, peaceful. He envied the stable boy.

"That Hines fella treated her like a dog," Wiley said.

To Valero's chagrin, the boy had followed him.

Wiley stood with anticipation, his eyes bright.

"She used to be a pretty gal. Only roan coat we got in here."

"She's still a pretty gal," Valero said.

He ran his hand—sore from gripping the shovel—through her mane. The crust was gone from her hair. There was a silkiness to it.

"You oughta see the scars she's got on her hindquarters. He kept her in a damned shed. Surprised she ain't savage."

"Good heart. The boy did all that?"

Wiley shook his head.

"The old man did it to her," he said. "Felix was a waif. Hell, I coulda beat up on Felix. Bennie Wolf did it daily. Felix's old man was wicked in his own right."

Valero said nothing.

"Yes, sir. My old man worked with Bryson Hines. He was a real cuss. Pa wouldn't've gone with that posse if not for Cora and Willa. He told me so before he left. That's why I didn't go. I mean, if you're wonderin'."

"Your name Wiley?"

"Yes, sir. How'd you come by that information?"

"Ryder."

"Good source. Ain't nothin' he don't know."

"That ain't true. There's something you and him neither one knows."

"What's that?" the boy asked.

"How to shut the hell up."

Wiley stared.

"I'm gonna hammer your head to the wall if you don't give me some quiet."

"Yes, sir."

As Wiley turned to go, he stopped cold at the sight of three shadows standing in the livery doorway. The timbre of the room shifted, and suddenly the darkness was gloomy.

One of the trio said, "There he is. By God, that's him. One and the same."

Maureen shook free of Valero's touch. She retreated into the stall.

Wiley walked to the front of the barn with a timidity that belied his character.

Valero watched. To Maureen, he said, "Don't you worry, gal."

The horse paid no heed. At the first note of tension, she began the laborious task of turning in her stall.

"It sure as hell is," another man said.

The third, with a grunt in his throat, agreed.

"Hi, fellas," Wiley said. He was guarded. The men were not to his liking. They had bad intentions. "What's your pleasure, friends?"

"Remove yourself," one of the men ordered.

"Go play in the river," said another.

Dutifully, Wiley stepped aside.

"Eli Valero. Now that's a name I've heard of. You heard it, Grant?"

"I've been made aware of it, yep."

"Dirk?"

The third man grunted assent.

Valero stepped from the stall. A twin thought, double-edged, was foremost in his mind. The Colt in his jacket was loaded, and the trio bore no sign of wearing guns. Valero walked forward, as did the men. The one named Dirk lifted Wiley's sickle from the chair as he passed.

Wiley watched him do so, and his face drained of color.

Valero was not alone. From the darkness of Maureen's stall, he sensed the delicate movement of a Spider.

The men came together in the center of the barn, with their backs to the sunlight. Valero scanned their faces. These were brutish men, but they weren't killers. None of the men carried a gun, not openly. If a gun were in their possession, it would be a hidden Derringer. These men were accustomed to bludgeoning and hammering with their fists. It was the only way they knew to fight. The man with a sickle held it for intimidation. The way he held the tool indicated he couldn't use it to slice meat from bone.

These were simpletons.

Be careful lest they beguile you, said the Spider.

"I heard of you," Grant said. His mouth was full of tobacco, and he spat gobs into the loam. He shifted the wad of chew from one jaw to the other. Brown juice gathered at his lips.

Valero said nothing. He watched, poised.

"I hear the lunch bell," Wiley said from inside one of the stalls. "They're filing out of Rand's right now. Goin' back to work. Y'all better get movin'."

The men ignored him.

"Me, Dirk, and Jeremiah here was just talkin' 'bout you," Grant said. "Me and Dirk saw you this mornin' with a shovel and pick." His breath was hard with liquor. He had a swimming look in his eyes. "Hell, I was in Ellenwood when you killed that Army sergeant. I saw you do it."

"Was he fast?" Jeremiah asked.

Grant shook his head. "Fast enough. Real calm. Newspaper man said he had eyes like an 'undisturbed lake'." He laughed. "I got a kick outta that."

"An undisturbed lake?" Dirk said. He laughed.

Grant peered into Valero's face. "Look a little stormier these days."

"I heard you killed damn near thirty men," Jeremiah said.

"And a few women and boys," Dirk added. He twisted the sickle.

"I heard you was in a hospital for lunatics. That right? Is that what it does when you have that much blood on your hands? Get a bunch of ghosts in your head?"

"Look at him. He's confused all to hell."

"I'll say he ain't the specimen I heard tale of in stories," Jeremiah said. "A little scrawny. Hard times, maybe."

"Kindly move aside," Valero said.

Do they not look familiar? the Spider asked. *Do you not know these faces?*

"Son," Grant said, "you oughta know we came in here for one purpose only, and that's to whup your ass."

"I ain't had someone talk to me like that in a long time," Valero said.

"That so?"

With no more than a tick of the shoulder, Valero drew the Colt Navy. He aimed the barrel from a position low at his waist. His first shot would rend Dirk's stomach.

"Throw it down," Valero said, nodding at the sickle.

With hooded eyes, Dirk dropped the blade.

"Nothin' but a coward with a gun," he said. "We ain't got guns."

"You had to have two partners to say that," Valero said.

"Easy now," Grant said. "We came with the express purpose of whuppin' your ass, but we ain't, have we? No reason to throw that thing around."

"Fuckin' lunatic," Dirk muttered.

Valero looked at Grant, but his gun was trained on Dirk's gut.

Grant said, "We thought maybe it wasn't Felix Hines that killed his folks. We thought maybe it was you. Odd a murderer like you would be in town at a time like that."

Jeremiah, from Valero's left, made his move. He'd planned his action too long, though, and his face telegraphed his intentions. As he closed his fist, Valero swung the Colt and fired.

The horses went mad at the explosion of the revolver, confined as it was in the stable.

In the atmosphere of stomping pandemonium, with Wiley scaling the wall, three men stood relatively motionless: Valero with a warm gun, the other two frozen.

Jeremiah doubled at the waist, a bullet having torn through his gut and smashed in a crumpled ball at his right hipbone. In agony, he fell to his knees. He clutched at the blood, trying to stop it. His hands were red. His lips went purple. Jeremiah was too shocked to speak, although his mouth trembled.

Valero aimed the gun between Grant and Dirk. Neither moved. Disbelief stayed on their faces. They watched their buddy, Jeremiah. He fell against his shoulder and writhed in the dirt. He moaned, the way men do when a bullet hits bone.

This was not how men fought in Bone-of-Wellington.

"You killed him," Grant said feebly. His face was white. "We ain't got any guns," he said, as if that meant something.

"Who are you really?" Valero asked.

The Spider formed his question. He felt her presence on the desert of his tongue. She crawled, he realized, from his stomach. She inched towards his lips. Valero nearly asked the men to produce their rope, the noose they'd brought along.

Was the hanging to be here? From the rafters?

"You sonnuva bitch," Dirk said.

Misplaced pride moved him. He lurched for the sickle at his feet.

Valero shot off the top of his skull as he bent forward, a glancing blow like a rock skipping across water. The bullet ended in the stable wall. Dirk was unconscious before he hit the ground, shrouding the sickle beneath his bulk. Brain seeped through a red patch in his hair.

Grant stood alone. Instinctively, he raised his hands, a defenseless man.

Valero centered his gun. He had to control the hot-blooded rush. He didn't want his hand to shake.

"Please," Grant said. "We got families." Proximity to death made panic rise in his voice. He trembled with it.

"Then I'd be more careful."

Valero pulled the trigger a third time.

A bullet tore through Grant's knee, shattering bone. The man crumpled like an empty sack. He grabbed the wound and screamed. Between the horses and Grant, the noise in the stable was deafening.

"Please, Jesus," Grant said.

He'll kill you when you sleep, the Spider whispered. *He'll come after you if you let him live. This isn't finished.*

He'll kill you when you sleep.

In the street, a crowd gathered. Wiley clambered over the stall, wild-eyed. The horses went mad. Outwardly, Valero appeared calm, but inside he was turbulent. He hesitated, which was something he would not have done in his youth. Hesitation got men killed.

Shock kept the violence from registering with the men who amassed at the door of the stable. Being simple, their first thought was an accident, not murder, but seeing a man standing with a gun while three lay on the ground would not take long to sink in.

Kill him, she said.

There was no time. He had to run.

Kill him, she demanded.

Valero looked to the back wall of the stable. There was a door, closed with a block of wood that turned loosely on a nail.

Kill him.

He had to run. The men started forward as Wiley spouted off about what he witnessed.

Kill him.

Valero couldn't take it. The Spider wouldn't stop. As he aimed his Colt, he locked eyes with Grant. The man didn't deserve to die, regardless of his stupidity, but that's not the way the dice landed. Valero mashed the trigger, shooting Grant through the neck. Blood erupted like vomit from the man's mouth. The sight reminded Valero of an opening blossom.

The other men jumped back at the shot.

Pleased, the Spider stilled.

Valero sprinted to the back door, gripping the revolver. He glanced back, not at the men but at poor Maureen. He turned the block of wood, freed the door, and fled into the sunlight.

TALL red cedars, some straight as poles and others with bent spines, lined the road and joined in a loose canopy above. The sun fell behind the trees. Yews and spruces coated the forest with a deep shade of green. With novelty it was arresting to the eye, but after miles the tableau induced sleep. A breeze moved through, carrying whiffs of pine that blended with the roiling decay of the wagon.

Without interruption or the prying eyes of travelers, the funeral procession rolled on. Felix rode a lean pinto, brown at the face with large swaths of white at her neck and back. The horse belonged to the Wolf family. Some of Bennie's belongings, mainly a knife and ammunition, remained in the saddlebags. Felix had to adjust the stirrup to ride with comfort, but the mare was a good fit.

Corbin rode ahead of the wagon on a red-shaded steed, while Spence slouched on the buckboard, reins in one hand, a cigarette burning in the other. For once, he wore his battered hat rather than hanging it around his neck. Two draft horses with broad backs pulled the ghastly cargo. Corbin had found a canvas tarpaulin among the men's supplies, and he stretched it over the bodies to blanket the worst of the smell. Miasma seeped through the fabric.

Felix surmised that the posse brought the tarpaulin as a body bag. Perhaps it was meant for him, to escort him to town once he'd been captured and hanged. It was pleasing to look upon the reversal of roles. The sight gave him a sense of vindication. Felix was content, even happy.

———•◆•———

Under the canvas, beneath the weight of dead meat, every breath was poisonous. The air he breathed was repulsively organic, clouded like sewage. Thoughts stirred and memories burned. Hector Bray awakened. His confusion was that of a newborn. All was dark, the heat was intense, and a barrage of stench, noise, and agony assaulted him. He focused on the clank of wagon springs, the clop of horses, and crow caws that issued from the woods in triplets. The birds spoke in the wind, flying between trees.

Hector tried to imagine the birds, but it was a cornfield in his mind, not a forest. Stalks moved in the breeze. A crow called its triad. Another answered. Another, now closer. The brittle leaves on the stalks had a sound all their own, a tapping more than a rustling. The cornfield spread out like a sea, a maze of rows. The birds cast black shadows on the field as they crossed. A dark-haired woman walked in the field, her pinned hair, soft beneath a bonnet, rising above the stalks.

Hector recognized the woman.

He concentrated. With grit alone, he kept from fainting. He had to string together enough thoughts to be alive, to be human. He breathed miasma until it lacquered his throat. Then he thought of Constance, because it was she who walked in the field, and an anger swelled in him that made his head lighten. There was a child on her hip, a toddler with hair like the corn silk. The baby reached out and touched the hard, tapping leaves of the cornstalks and giggled. Constance laughed.

He could not die. He steeled himself, but the surge of emotion was too much. With no blood to spare, Hector blacked out.

———◆———

Laconically, Spence answered, "They'll burn."

"What about Pierce Ryder?"

"Corbin has ways of makin' 'em talk. He has a knack for it."

"Ryder isn't a bad old guy," Felix said.

"He's a brown nose. I can imagine how bruised his knees are from dealin' with the Argos."

"I s'pose," Felix replied.

"How easy does he live? How else you get another man payin' you a salary like that?" As was normal with Spence's temperament, he grew angry in an instant. Blood flushed his cheeks.

"He's poor enough."

"So he looks."

"What are you going do with your silver?" Felix asked.

Spence shrugged. He fell silent, scowling at the reins.

Dusk approached. The sun dipped low. In the darkness of the woods, the call of an owl reverberated. Felix looked up to find something of an owls' lair, with several large nests filling the joints of the trees. He counted the nests as he passed below.

Growing tired, Felix imagined the sight of Bone-of-Wellington on fire, the hulking mill steeped in smoke.

ELIJAH held the gun rigidly, a silhouette in the basin of the dry creek. Shamefully, the boy did nothing. Only his eyes moved. Terror consumed his intuition, buried his thoughts. He stood there, only to be moved by the force of another.

His mother lay quietly on the road, her pale skin exposed in the darkness. She wore not a shred of clothing. Her face was turned away from him, but he'd seen the contortion of her features. Although she'd fought with demonic fury, she did not move now. She did not berate. Her sickness was not apparent. She was quiet.

The Hangman navigated stones along the bank. Gravel crunched beneath his boots. He was immense. He carried the noose, twirling it playfully, broadening the loop and closing it. He approached the boy.

Elijah smelled the septic quality of his breath. He had blood on his fingertips. His shirt was ripped, and the fabric hung open at his neck. His own blood covered his chest where Elijah's mother raked him.

The Hangman spoke, but the boy was too stricken to hear. The voice was no more in his mind than the owls and crickets in the woods. His thoughts closed around the man before him, and the image was carved into his mind.

With miniscule effort, a squeeze of the wrist, the Hangman stole the gun from the boy's grasp. He opened the chamber and emptied bullets into his palm. He threw the gun into a scum-crusted pool. He pocketed the bullets.

He knelt, and the Hangman was face-to-face with Elijah. He wore a grey beard. His eyes were dull orbs in the shadow. He was not a poor man. His business was steady. This time, when he spoke, the words penetrated.

"If you speak a word," the Hangman said, "I'll be back for you."

He raised the noose, draping it over his massive hand like a snake. He showed the boy how it would fit around his neck, how it would constrict.

"Who are you?" the boy asked.

"Just a graveyard ghost," the man said. "Run home, little one."

"What did you do?" Elijah asked.

The Hangman turned his back. He walked to his mount.

"What'd you do to her?" the boy screamed.

The Hangman put a finger to his lips.

Elijah went to his mother, kneeling at her side. She was a broken doll. His grief was so complete that he stayed in that position, sitting in the dirt and touching her hair, until dawn brought another horse and traveler. It was the most complete feeling he'd ever known. The boy was exhausted from a night without sleep and hours of crying. His face was swollen and blank.

"Good God," the man said.

"I'll kill him," Elijah told the traveler. "When I see him again, I'll kill him."

"Child, raise up." In pity, the man took his arm. "Quiet now," he said.

"I'll kill him."

"Quiet now, child. Be calm."

VALERO dashed up an incline to the railroad tracks. To his left stood a platform, a crude depot gilded with sunlight, and to his right the sawmill towered over the riverside, the color of a wasp's nest. Voices filled the stable below, but they were as tangled and incomprehensible as Valero's thoughts. More men filed out of the mill, heading towards the commotion. A stream of people emerged. A few women and children wandered in from the shanties. The stable buzzed like a hive. Ryder, Sophia, and Constance came running. Anger, curiosity, or a mix of both drove them.

Amassed, the population of Bone-of-Wellington didn't look so small.

Valero crossed the tracks, trying to harness his thoughts. If only he had Maureen ready, he'd take her and flee. He didn't, and now the crowd blocked in the horse. Valero leapt the rail. A mad rush of ideas deepened his confusion. He shoved the gun into his coat, then he removed the weapon just as quickly. He emptied the four spent chambers.

After rushing into the tree line that butted the far edge of the tracks, he slid fresh bullets into the Colt. He wrapped the hard bones of his fingers around the gun like roots.

Valero breathed in. From his position in the shadow, he no longer saw the stable, but he heard the buzzing crowd. He stood in a grove of red cedars, the lifeblood of the mill, of these people. He stood exposed, visible to anyone who crossed the tracks.

There was little chance the people would call his actions self-defense. The men he killed were unarmed.

If you let them near enough, they'll try to arrest you. You'll have to kill more of them to get free.

Where are you now? he thought.

He reached into his mouth and groped for the Spider, but she was gone. Angrily, Valero withdrew his hand. He had the urge to crush her. She was always there to urge and prod, but she was never there to comfort. Her abandonment caused deep resentment.

Once she had come to him in a forest like this, a monstrosity balanced in the crook of a tree limb. He wished she would come again, despite the terror she manifested. Valero implored until begging became a prayer.

The branches above waited empty. The floor of needles remained undisturbed.

He was alone.

Like a pursued animal, Valero sprinted hard into the wilderness. The trees passed in a blur. He ran without looking back, crashing through the bramble, swiping briars with the barrel of his gun, raking his body with those he missed. Valero ran until stitches in his side grew unbearable. When he stopped, he gulped at the air. He aimed his Colt at the trees. He would've shot anything that moved, but nothing did. He managed his breath, slowing it, until he could hear properly. The only noise from the woods was natural, the high thrumming of summer.

Where are you? he begged. *What do I do?*

He went to his knees, and he clawed at a bed of clover and mulch. Had she crawled below? He believed she had, although he forgot the precise moment when he saw her do so. He found nothing except writhing earthworms.

She was not here. Had she burrowed? He dug deeper, shoveling away handfuls of earth.

Where are you? he demanded. *Show yourself.*

He threw the dirt as he clutched it. He knew she was here. He had never been so driven in his life.

At some point, he put down his gun. Immersed, panicked, desperate, Valero didn't hear the approach of four paws through the brush. Sophia, cowed by Valero's bizarre and frantic energy, moved to his side with caution. Her head was down. She did not want to anger him. She nudged his boot politely, requesting attention.

Valero stopped digging. He turned to see the dog.

She's leading them to you, the voice said. *She betrayed you.*

Sophia edged closer.

Valero looked at his gun in the dirt.

No, he thought then. *There's nothing wicked in her heart.*

He tried to calm himself. He glanced at the hole he was digging. No Spider crawled from the soil.

Delicately, Valero picked up Sophia from the ground, cradling her. The dog panted, but she didn't protest. He felt her quick heartbeat. He stroked her head and scratched her ears, and, as he did, his mind cleared. He was whole, if only briefly.

More steps then. Heavier, clumsier. A voice followed.

"Elijah? Elijah, you up here?"

Valero maintained reason. He gripped Sophia tighter.

It's Ryder, he thought. *It's not an imitation of Ryder. It's Ryder. It's not an imitation of Ryder. It's Ryder. Be calm.*

The old man appeared, struggling through briars. Gnats swarmed the brim of his hat.

"Atta girl," Ryder said, grinning at the dog. "That's my baby."

"Who's with you?" Valero asked.

Ryder checked over his shoulder. He shrugged.

"Just me. Honest. They aren't eager to follow. Not after that mess down there."

Valero listened to be certain. When he was satisfied that Ryder was alone, he nodded.

"Got a gun on you?" Valero asked.

Ryder shook his head.

"No gun. Nothin'." He watched Valero's face for a reaction. "Can I sit with you?"

His eyes locked with those of the old man, but Valero said nothing.

Ryder took that as an affirmative. He shuffled nearer and sat on the dirt. He glanced around Valero and Sophia.

"You diggin' a hole? Or was it her?" He smiled.

Valero released the dog. He found nothing humorous in the situation. Sophia remained at his side rather than returning to Ryder. She lay on the ground and panted. A full minute passed before another word was spoken.

Ryder asked, "What happened down there, Elijah?"

"What always happens," Valero said. "They tried to corner me." His anger swelled. He'd provoked none of this.

"You got a reputation. That why?"

Valero said nothing. He petted the dog. Animals were easier to deal with than people. He lifted her into his lap.

"Wiley said they started it."

The silence dragged.

"Hey, you hear me? He said you didn't do anything to anybody. Not everybody's buyin' that just now, but Wiley was the only one to see it. He right?"

"What a kid says doesn't mean shit."

"Is he right or wrong, Elijah?"

"If they try to hang me, I'll kill 'em all. Including you."

"Nobody's tryin' to hang you."

"Hell."

Ryder gathered himself together. He was, Valero sensed, nervous. He was frightened.

"You got good in you," the old man said. "You know that? That pup knows it." He pointed at Sophia. "Maureen knows it. I do, too. Even Connie knows it."

Valero stared into the woods. The gnats and flies were thick.

"You know what she said about you this morning? She came lookin' to apologize for last night. She said she senses some of her husband in you."

"How the hell's that a compliment?"

Ryder smiled.

"Okay, well, she apologized."

Valero stroked Sophia. The dog looked up at him, panting.

"Believe it or not, I've read about you. That book talked about you like a hero. I remember that much. Said all the good things you did to help people. You got sick after that, didn't you? You got sick, and you can't stop being sick. Is that right?"

Valero's breath shook. He tried to control himself. Scratching the dog helped.

"You feel like everybody's out to get you, don't you? You're always looking over your shoulder."

"They are out to get me. He is."

"Who is?"

Valero stopped short of mentioning the Hangman. He couldn't unpack those feelings in front of another man. He refused.

Ryder persisted, "Who's out to get you?"

Valero was silent.

"It's okay to be sick, Elijah. There are places, big hospitals, that can help you."

"I'm a lunatic," Valero said.

"To an extent, yes," Ryder said.

Valero stared.

"But you're not gone. You can be brought back. You wanna come back with me?"

"No."

"What are you gonna do?"

"Prob'ly steal your dog. Knock you over the head. Steal that horse. Be on my way after that."

Ryder laughed, but it was forced.

Valero didn't laugh.

"Better than it could be," Ryder said. "How 'bout you do all that tomorrow?"

"I step in that town they'll fall in on me. I'll kill everyone of 'em that tries it."

Ryder didn't argue.

"Tell you what. There's a shack for loggers about a mile up. It's all rot 'cause it ain't used anymore, but it's shelter. Would you stay there tonight and talk to me in the morning?"

"Then those assholes corner me. I ain't in the mood to get beat up on."

"No, they won't. I won't say a word. You're as good as gone."

"Why help me?"

"Seems like the right thing to do. Besides, I like you."

"Despite that?" Valero gestured at the town below.

"That's hard to swallow—death means a little more to me than it does you—but, yeah, despite that."

Valero nodded assent. In truth, he hadn't the energy to flee. He still hadn't recovered from digging graves, let alone his time in the monastery.

"One thing," Valero said.

"What's that?"

"I keep your dog with me."

Ryder grimaced.

"You wouldn't really steal her, would you? I need her, too. That's my girl."

"No," Valero admitted. "It's only for the night. I got morals, believe it or not."

"Talk about havin' a tiger by the goddamn tail," Ryder said.

BATS swooped towards the river, chasing insects, a ritual of summer. The bats journeyed from an escarpment in a hill beyond town each evening at dusk. Bats would fill the sky, darting with grace, sniping at prey. From a distance the choreography was elegant, but up close the bats were hideous as rodents, veined wings of brown-black, tufts of dark hair.

Work at the mill ground to a halt. Some men filed into Rand's, while others streamed towards the shanties. The men did not talk seriously about forming another posse, although a great many of them spoke of Eli Valero and Felix Hines, killers close to their breast.

The first posse had been gone too long—of that, too, they spoke. Of that, they worried. The men in the posse, Hector Bray included, were not so dedicated that they would remain long in the field. Something was wrong.

Three more bodies. Three more coffins. Three more graves on the hill above the Kinnikinnick River.

A nervous energy pervaded Bone-of-Wellington. There was a fear of becoming complacent in the face of carnage. Men questioned why they hadn't followed Eli Valero.

Was it complacency? Or was it fear? Which was worse?

It was as though the delicate skin of civilization had been peeled away from their settlement.

Thinking like this led to copious drinking. Rand's would stay busy through the night.

The people in town ignored the prosaic sight of bats over the river.

Like a goddamned animal, one the men said.

Such brutality, said another man.

You think he's out there waiting?

You think he'll come back?

Maybe we should put together some men.

More drinking than volunteering followed.

In the shanties, spouses talked deep into the night.

Such brutality.

Where did it come from?

———◆———

High on the hill, sitting in a wooden chair outside the cabin's front door, Valero watched bats flying over the river. Mosquitoes gnawed at the sweat on his scalp. Calmly, but repeatedly, he brushed them away.

The air inside the cabin was stuffy and hot. The spartan interior reminded him of one of the monk cells at the monastery, and he didn't welcome the connection. Thoughts of the monastery triggered nothing but shame.

Valero had a restored sense of clarity. He made peace with killing the three men below. He experienced no guilt. His mind was quiet about the matter. He approached calm, although the gulf was far.

As yet, no men had followed in pursuit. Pierce Ryder kept his word.

Sophia sniffed the air and patrolled the grass. She did the most to calm him. He enjoyed watching the dog, seeing an animal that could experience joy. She played the role of guardian, and it was a self-appointed role. Occasionally, the dog grew bored with patrolling and whined for Valero's attention.

When he snapped his fingers, she pranced closer. She flopped on her back. He bent at the waist to scratch her belly.

A bull snake slithered past, not an inch short of four feet, but Sophia was oblivious to the intruder, enjoying the belly scratch with eyes closed.

Some guardian, Valero thought, and he laughed.

IN the moonlight, Felix walked through sand at the river's edge until he met with the lapping water. Tonight the water was slow, almost still, and stank of fish. Oil varnished the surface. The water looked like a mirror of obsidian. Ahead, the river quickened its pace where the sawmill loomed, and cataracts broke the water into streams.

Felix stripped his clothes and stepped into the current. Mud was like slime beneath his feet. He walked until the water reached his waist. Frightfully cold, he wrapped his arms around his skeletal chest, gripping his shoulders. He reached a precipice, beyond which the riverbed dipped ten feet or more. Felix stood in the soft current. Folding his legs, he submerged. He opened his eyes below but saw nothing in the darkness. The water was fully black.

Holding his breath, he scrubbed at his hair and face, washing away grime. He emerged, breaking the skin of the water, shattering a reflection of the yellow moon, and he gasped. The cold shocked his brain.

Felix wondered again if the Kinnikinnick led to the ocean. He wondered where its current would lead him. It was pure romance, but his desire to see the ocean intensified. The conjoined howl of coyotes, emanating from a hill on the opposite shore, brought him back to the night's reality.

The thrill of the task ahead made Felix shudder harder than the cold.

He tramped through the muck, returning to the shoreline. As his pale form surfaced, he noticed that a couple of leeches had attached to his inner thigh. With disgust, he pinched away their slimy forms. He threw them towards the bank. Blood trickled at his leg, twin wounds, which he patted away with the water. Once on the shore, he crushed the leeches with a broad stone.

As Felix dressed, Corbin and Spence emerged from the forest. The men talked in agitated tones, and they cradled limbs that would be used for torches. There was a detail in their plan over which they'd argued for the past hour. From their looks, it appeared Spence got his way.

The wagon, its cargo draped with canvas, stood alone. The horses were fettered to trees, making a meal of the grass around their legs. A nighthawk, competing with the bats for insects, cut the night with its staccato call. Bone-of-Wellington, a hill away, had no impact on the night. It was silent, dark, fully asleep.

Spence went to the horses and wagon, depositing the limbs he carried. Corbin did the same, but, once free of the burden, he walked to meet Felix. Languidly, Corbin scanned Felix's wet clothes and hair. It was an unsettling effect seeing his eye work so hard to cover a scene while the other looked like a stillborn fetus in his skull.

"You know the town better than either of us," Corbin said. "We got somethin' for you to do." He paused. "What the hell you doin' in the water?"

"I was overwrought," Felix said. "I had to calm down."

Corbin thought to himself, then he said, "We'll get everything to the edge of town, then you go in and scope it out. If it's clear, we'll head on."

Felix's stomach sank.

"They'll know me," he protested.

"I was hopin' you'd be quiet enough not to trumpet your arrival, kid. Keep your fuckin' face down. Besides, there ain't gonna be no sentinel on a gate."

Felix nodded, but he had another reason to be nervous.

"I'm ready," he said.

Corbin started back to the wagon.

Felix followed.

"The wagon's for the morning," Spence whispered.

With the grace of a thief, he rose from the buckboard, deposited the reins, and stepped gently to the road. If he made any noise doing so, the horses covered it with their shifting.

Corbin, with less grace, led three horses into a grove of red cedars. Out of sight from the road, he tied off the animals. The horses snorted in protest, but they offered no further resistance. Corbin returned. He frowned at the wagon.

"Just leave it where it is," Spence said.

Apparently, this was one of the sore points between the men, but Felix was too anxious to care. His palms sweated. If recognized, walking back into Bone-of-Wellington would be like walking into the lions' den. They'd tear him limb from limb. The danger also brought excitement. If he could only still his heart—it thundered heavy as a drum.

Spence approached.

"Head down," he ordered. "Peek between the buildings in case they got somebody standin' guard. I doubt it, but you need to check."

"Got it."

"You nervous?" Spence chuckled.

Felix nodded once, curtly.

"We'll have the torches ready when you get back. You got a gun?"

"I do. And this." Felix raised the machete.

"Good. Hop to."

Felix did as he was told. He started down the slope towards Bone-of-Wellington. The settlement spread out darkly before the river, couched in a mist that hugged the ground. There were few lamps to illuminate the streets, footpaths, and alleys. The only lights were two candles that burned in lamps on the front porch of Rand's Hotel. The lamps hung from the awning, creaking when a breeze off the river moved them. The lamps were unattended, present as a welcoming note to travelers who arrived under the cover of night.

Gripping the machete, his mouth dry with fear, Felix started through Main Street. He kept away from the chains. He walked past the mortuary shed and home of Pierce Ryder. The windows were dark, hushed. He walked to the office of Hector Bray.

It was odd, dreamlike, to be in town again. When so many wanted him dead, walking freely felt powerful.

Felix moved down a narrow passage between stores and looked upon twin rows of shanties. He walked to the home of his mother and father, and he stood outside. A feeling of control, an exceptional feeling, washed over him. He spent too many years of his life in this hole. It represented nothing but misery. Now the shack was forlorn, and the door hung open. The salt of violence emanated from inside.

With pride, Felix looked at the surrounding homes.

If you'd known, he thought, *you wouldn't have fucked with me.*

The cemetery rose behind the shanties. Felix didn't take time to search further. He was satisfied that no one was awake, that no one guarded the town. Bidding farewell to the home he'd always known, and always despised, he returned to Corbin and Spence.

CORBIN led the way to the graveyard. It was a corner of the settlement with which Felix was intimately familiar. Even in the darkness, he recognized the solemn features: the fence, the gate, the stones placed without care. He had read of the Egyptians and their slavish devotion to the dead. What a contrast their monuments made with this patch of unkempt weeds. As a boy, he often took the books he borrowed from Ryder to the cemetery. He liked to sit in the grass and prop his back against a fence pole. The place was quiet, bordered in the rear by forest, and it possessed a good view of the river.

At the far left of the cemetery, Felix spotted three graves covered in loose dirt. Unadorned graves. Ryder had yet to place stones in memoriam. Looking at them, remembering, made him proud. He wanted to make tonight a recreation of that night. His grip tightened on the machete.

Corbin put his foot on the fence and looked down. He let Felix have his moment, then he called the boy over.

"How's it look, kid?" he asked.

Felix peered at the shacks and their pitiful, tar-spattered rooftops. Spence was barricading one of the front doors. He worked quietly.

"Can you fuckin' imagine how Old Man Argo lives?" Corbin asked.

Felix had seen Argo and his entourage. The man reeked of opulence.

"He has a diamond-encrusted cigarette case," Felix whispered. "And servants no better than slaves. He used to keep slaves."

Corbin nodded as Felix spoke.

"Imagine if you put his home, God knows what it's fuckin' like, in the middle of this shithole. All that money beside these puny fuckin' shacks. Must be somethin' to be a rich ol' bastard. I bet he likes seein' these fuckin' assholes in misery. Hell, I sure would."

"You're right. Why else would he bury silver here? It's all a big joke to him."

"Imagine their fuckin' faces when they find out," Corbin said. "It'll kill 'em. To be workin' on a silver lode all this time and not fuckin' know it."

When Spence walked up the hill, Corbin prepared the torches for lighting. The limbs were wrapped at the top with strips of a flannel sheet doused in kerosene.

"Who'd you lock in?" Felix asked.

Spence shrugged.

"Just a couple. They'll be burned pretty good before they get out."

"Not Bray's old lady?" Corbin asked.

"Hell no. I wouldn't mar that body. I plan on enjoyin' it."

"Fuckin' amen to that."

"That whole goddamn row is soaked in kerosene. Set a torch to the door and they'll go up like matchsticks. Felix, you start at the far end. Corbin, you start at the base of the hill. I'll be up here with the rifles. You get 'em loaded?"

Corbin pointed at two Winchesters propped against the fence.

"They're ready," he said.

"Watch the heat," Spence cautioned.

Felix grabbed a torch from the grass. He said nothing, but he knew who Spence had locked in. The hilarity of it made him smile. It was the home of Jim Packard and his wife. Packard was the foreman under whom Felix worked, as had Corbin and Spence. Spence remembered where he lived all this time.

"Got matches?" Corbin whispered.

Starting down the hillside, Felix nodded. He had a pocketful.

He had no sense of time in the darkness. Satisfied he was alone, Hector summoned all the strength left in his body, clamped his mouth, and began the arduous task of clawing through a mound of flesh.

He squirmed loose from a corpse that mashed his hips. He lurched in pain with each exertion. His mind was delirious with agony. With grit, he kept his mind on the image of Constance and the child. He would move, pause until the pain lessened, then move again. Three corpses covered his body, and he moved each. Pushing aside a hand, an arm, a shoulder at a time. With a foot he could control, Hector propelled himself upward. He was numb to the stench and taste.

With a gasp, he reached the canvas.

All it took was the slightest contact, an extension of the torch, and flame spread across the façade.

There were six shacks on each side of the road, including the one barricaded with a forked limb at the doorjamb. The folks inside slept, oblivious. Felix lit three shanties in quick succession, sprinting up the line. Fire spread from the base of the door to the roof in less than a second. The sound reminded Felix of a sheet in the wind. As the flames became a towering wall, a destructive roar emerged. Smoke roiled into the sky. When flames met the tar-coated roofs, the fire leapt even higher.

Felix threw his torch into the road and ran towards the graveyard. He assumed Corbin followed. When he reached the path, however, flushed with exhilaration, he turned to see. Corbin remained in the street, the torch burning in his grasp. From the look on Corbin's face, this amounted to the greatest thrill of his life. He absorbed each second.

From inside the shanties, screams and shouts erupted.

At this, Corbin discarded his torch and ran to towards the path.

Men, women, and children threw open their doors. The men raised a cry for help. Men carried leather pails. A simple ordinance of Bone-of-Wellington in action: the mandatory fire brigade.

"Get to the river," one of the men shouted, and the futility was comical to Felix.

A man laden with pails ran towards the distant water.

Felix and Corbin made it to the graveyard. Spence stood at the fence with a rifle at his shoulder. He'd yet to fire. His face glowed with light from the flames.

Heroically, the doors of the burning shanties burst open. One by one, hulks in wet blankets emerged, cutting through the flames in desperation. There were shouts of agony as they shed the burning blankets and hit the streets. One man dragged his child out the door, and the boy's trousers caught fire, fabric accelerating the blaze. He fell on the child in an attempt to put out the fire. Instead, he ignited, too.

Corbin laughed so hard that he doubled over the fence.

Then there was the home of Jim Packard. The door shuddered several times as he attempted to open it. Too much time passed. The window shattered. His wife flew out the window as if she'd been thrown. Blackened, Packard struggled through the opening. His wife lay where she fell. Packard slumped over the windowsill. His back was burning.

Flames rose fifty feet into the sky, casting a gleam on the somber river, reaching higher than the graveyard.

The entire town stood in the street, gilded by firelight. The man with the pails had yet to return with water.

Corbin went to Spence's side and lifted the other rifle.

"Now's good," Spence said.

He and Corbin fired into the crowd.

Mesmerized by the immense heat (even at this distance it felt as though his skin were burning, his hair singeing), Felix experienced a swell of wonder.

"Three," Spence shouted, counting the fallen. "Four."

Towards the sawmill, the sky rained embers. Smoke joined the clouds.

"Five."

"Six."

"Seven."

Hector fell from the back of the wagon, crashing hard against the road. He expected the pain, and he'd determined not to be frightened by it. This, he believed, would keep him from fainting.

The air was pungent with heavy, black smoke. As the smoke raked his lungs, Hector was refreshed. Smoke cleansed the decay that clung to his sinuses.

The horses stirred anxiously.

When the pain of the fall ebbed, Hector crawled inside a bank of weeds, free of the road, free of the wagon, the cadavers, free of Felix, Corbin, and Spence.

Relief withered when it dawned on him that Bone-of-Wellington was burning.

DAWN approached, and the black sky turned purple at the horizon. A chorus of eager birds replaced the crickets. Smoke billowed from the ruins. The stench of charred wood and flesh haunted the survivors who'd taken refuge at Rand's.

Ryder counted nineteen people. Most stood against the front windows, piling on one another, watching the street. It was a gallery of waifs. They were disheveled, pale, stricken with grief and fear, and their minds worked to process what had happened. The fires. The gunshots. Shock held sway.

Ryder stood among the crowd. The feeling in his gut reminded him of the war. The buzz in the air was that of absolute dread. He moved about, searching for Constance. In the preceding hours, she had grown convinced of Hector's death. Her expression oscillated between open despair and a stiff upper lip. She was close to shattering. Not knowing kept her miserable but knowing would wound her even deeper. Ryder wanted to be with Constance, to bring her some degree of comfort.

She was at the far window, away from the others, atop a table with her legs on the chair. She was fully dressed, which meant she hadn't tried to sleep the night prior. Her eyes were bloodshot from reading in lantern light. Constance gripped a handkerchief with ghostly hands. She nodded as Ryder approached.

What could be said?

He took her hand. He smiled wanly.

Constance looked through him, and then she returned her attention to the street.

Outside, eighteen lay dead. A few of the corpses were burned, the others opened by gunshot. Save for Jim Packard and his family, there was no discrimination in the killing. The night had unfolded as a game of chance.

As he had done many times that morning, Ryder wondered if Felix were capable of this. He had a personal motive, however deranged, for the patricide, but was the boy capable of the rage that preceded something like this? Ryder thought about Eli Valero, too, but he couldn't accept that either. He was torn. He was wrong about one of the men.

When the screams and shouts of fire had jarred him from sleep, Ryder had sprinted towards the shanties. By that juncture, flames had already stretched high. He'd arrived moments before gunfire erupted. In the melee, he'd spotted two silhouettes in the graveyard, firing down upon the crowd. Neither shape reminded him of Felix or Valero, but it was a judgment made in the face of chaos.

Several men in Rand's had guns, and they were determined to make the scene a standoff. Even in grief, their egos elbowed for space. They were not so weak as to be hobbled by cowards in the dark. So they boasted. They'd fight. Such talk was hubris. No one dared to set foot in the street. Standing near the window was brave enough.

In the end, Ryder wondered, where would they find the ammunition to fight? The only guns were those carried outside when the fires started. There was another gun behind Rand's bar, a pistol with two bullets in it. The gun belonged to Brigham Conway, a barkeep who was conspicuously absent from the throng. Either Conway hid elsewhere, which was doubtful, or he was among the dead.

When sunlight flushed the first floor of the hotel, spreading across a bar upon which women and children sat entangled, a clanging issued from the street. The mass pressed against the windows.

Lambs to the slaughter, Ryder thought.

"Get back," he shouted, but his admonishment was lost in the confused chatter.

The clanging was the wind chime of tin plates. Someone rattled it like a bell. The chimes were a note of introduction. Outside, led by familiar horses, a wagon covered in canvas rolled over the street chains. The wagon was a sorry-looking affair, coated in rust, with old farming utensils clasped on the sidewalls. No one drove the wagon. The buckboard was empty. There was a heavy cargo in the back, a mound testing the canvas. The horses halted before a set of cross-chains. The wagon rolled to a stop.

A man, whom Ryder recognized as Spence Hickman, stepped from an alley. He cradled a rifle. Behind him, another man aimed a rifle at Rand's, swinging his aim from window to window. Ryder recognized this man as Corbin Blum.

"Come greet your loved ones," Spence yelled, placing his hand at the edge of his mouth.

With a flourish, he stripped the wagon of its canvas tarpaulin. This was a punchline for which the man had worked hard.

"If you fire one goddamn shot, we'll kill each and every one of you," Hickman said. "Put the guns down. We got men with rifles all 'round. We'll torch you like we did those shacks, too. I wanna play fair."

The sight cowed even the strongest of the men. The murmur died, and silence hung over Rand's. After a few seconds, sobs from the women and children filled the air. It was clear from the clothes and horses that this was the posse that set out in search of Felix.

Constance Bray shouted in grief. She would have run through the window if it hadn't been for the restraining grasp of Ryder.

Flies swarmed the dead. Crusted fluids hardened at their orifices, like melting wax at the base of a candle. Their faces were haunting and distorted, with swollen eyes and open mouths. The proliferation of maggots was visible even from a distance. The writhing of worms gave the illusion of movement in some of the faces.

Ryder hadn't witnessed such wanton carnage since the war. It was horror incarnate. The sight made him tremble. He held Constance, pulling her against his chest as restraint rather than comfort.

He remembered Corbin and Spence, although not well. They had caused no trouble in their brief stay in Bone-of-Wellington. No serious trouble, at least. He only spoke to Corbin once, when the man inquired about Argo's legendary silver. Ryder told the man it was a children's story.

Again, Spence Hickman shouted.

"Claim your dead, goddamn it! Get out here!"

He and Corbin laughed, as did another, much smaller figure in their midst. Confounded, Ryder released Constance, and he pushed towards the glass for a better view. In the shadow stood Felix Hines.

Ryder's heart lurched.

"I'll take on the best of you one at a time," Spence said, "if you wanna do somethin' about it. Send out what you got."

A large man named Talbot, one of the few with a gun, volunteered. He took no time to decide. He ignored advice to remain sheltered. At the idea of testing Hickman, Talbot stood. He cracked his neck.

"Let me have a chance," he said to those around him. He was full of hate, irrational.

"Don't be a damn lunatic," Ryder said.

"You can shut the hell up," Talbot said, eyeing Ryder. "You already tried to protect that kid, you dumb sonnuva bitch bastard. He's right out there. You see him? You still wanna protect him? Sonnuva bitch fool."

The others, who'd yet to spot Felix, strained for a view. The room erupted at the sight.

"Gimme more bullets for this gun," Talbot said.

A man near Talbot handed over ammunition. Talbot loaded the weapon.

"Talbot," Ryder pleaded. "It'll make it worse. You're gonna get yourself goddamn killed."

"I don't see anybody else volunteering," Talbot countered.

No one proved him wrong. No one stopped him. Save for a few sobs, Rand's was quiet. Talbot took the gun and went to the batwing doors at the front of the building.

Without parting them, he shouted, "I'm comin' out." He waited.

Spence chuckled.

"You'll find the conditions fair," he said.

Talbot spread the door and walked into the sunlight. He stood on the porch, the gun dangling in his grip. Ryder wondered if Talbot expected to be shot then and there. The man had lost his mind. Grief and terror were capable of doing that.

Spence did not shoot, nor did Corbin.

Talbot walked into the street, a bevy of expectant faces over his shoulders. He trod on the chains and stopped when he was five feet from Spence. He had a shock of red hair that looked orange in the sun. Pocked with freckles, he stood firm, nearly six inches taller than Spence. He tightened his grip on the pistol.

"What'll it be?" Spence asked.

"How 'bout no guns?" Talbot said.

Ryder strained to hear. He was ashamed, but now that Talbot was in the street, he couldn't help but hope.

Spence nodded. He placed his rifle on the ground. He unbuckled a belt of ammunition at his waist. He pulled two pistols from the pockets of his jacket. When he was finished, artillery sufficient to arm several men lay in a pile.

Like a boxer, Spence loosened his shoulders and rolled his neck. His face was alight with joy.

He was too damned happy for Ryder's comfort. It was then that Ryder wished it were not a brute like Talbot in the street, but a killer like Elijah Valero. He was the one man capable of helping.

Talbot threw the punch of a brawler, a wide sweep of the arm. He was undisciplined and angry. Spence balled his fists, ducked the blow, and cracked a rib with his first punch. The blow knocked the air out of Talbot, and he nearly doubled over. His hands went down. To everyone watching it happened with the speed of a blink, but Spence was patient and measured. He threw a punch from the hip that slammed against Talbot's downturned face. There was a spray of blood.

To his credit, Talbot didn't go down. He jumped back, his face maroon and bleeding at his smashed nose. He made the mistake of turning his shoulder rather than facing Spence. It was instinctive. Spence tackled him. Talbot hit the chains with a fierce thud. When his neck snapped back, his head struck the earth. It dazed him, but he landed a few blows against Spence's neck and chin. Spence put his knee against Talbot's stomach, planting his bulk.

Talbot tried to roll him off but failed. He only managed to writhe and buck. Spence grabbed Talbot's red hair with one hand and hammered his skull with the other. He dropped the hair and pummeled with both fists.

The fight left Talbot. With one crushing blow against the side of Talbot's eye socket, a blow that trapped his skull between Spence's fist and the earth, the man's eye bulged, coming loose from the socket. The bulb protruded half an inch. After that blow, Talbot was unconscious.

Spence stood and straightened his walrus mustache. He had blood on his hands and across his shirt. Blood speckled his face. Playfully, he rubbed at his fist and shook his hand in the air. He pawed his neck, which was red from a few glancing punches.

"Nobody punches like a sawmill man," he said. "Like a mule kick."

"Next," Corbin said, laughing.

Spence went to the wagon and took a pick from the sidewall. His eyes lost their shine. He moved with the rote steps of a somnambulist. When he returned to Talbot's motionless form, he gripped the pick with both hands, and he hoisted it above his head. He looked like an executioner wielding his axe.

God, no, Ryder thought. A wave of despair overcame him.

Men clamored against the window, shouting into the street. The women pulled children against their chests, turning their heads.

"Just like the prison guard," Spence said, looking over his shoulder at Corbin.

"Damn close," Corbin replied.

With precision, he brought down the pick. Talbot's skull split wide, opening like a grotesque flower against the earth. His body shuddered, a rattle in his left foot, a rattle in his hands, and then he ceased to move. He urinated over the front of his trousers. He bled out over the chains. Spence left the pick planted in the bloody ground.

"That take the fuckin' fight out of you?" Corbin called. "Any more heroes among you? Or are you ready to talk?"

It was unclear when they had been unready to talk. Confusion spurred anger and fear within Rand's. This was all part of the game.

Another fool, Everett Thorn, split the batwing doors and rushed onto the front porch of the hotel. Madness drove him. He held a gun. No one saw him clamoring for the move, and no one was in a position to stop him. He didn't open his mouth, and he barely raised his gun, when Corbin Blum took aim and planted a shot in his chest. Thorn stumbled and fell forward against the railing. Blum approached with a pistol and blew open his skull. The spatter reached beneath the doors.

"How 'bout now?" he asked, close enough for the people to feel his presence.

"Don't anybody goddamned move," a man shouted, elevating himself above the crowd by climbing the stairwell. "Be sensible."

Ryder leaned close to Constance's ear. She clenched her jaw. Mentally, she had gone elsewhere. She was oblivious to what happened to Thorn. Ryder didn't like the cadaverous look on her face—achieving such a gaze left mental scars.

"Go get Elijah," Ryder said. "He's in the old logger cabin."

It took a moment for Constance to understand.

"Why?" she asked. Her voice was quiet, little more than a breath. She brought the handkerchief to her eyes and wiped, but there were no tears.

"Because he's a killer," Ryder said. "Unlike these fools."

Constance said nothing, but she pulled a cigarette from the front pouch of her dress. Ryder found a match and struck it.

"Just get to him, however you can."

She nodded.

"Ready to talk?" Corbin asked. "We wanna know one fuckin' thing. Somebody in here knows where Argo hid his fuckin' silver. Ain't that right?"

He stood beyond the batwing doors. His shadow crossed the floor.

"Send out the old man," he said. "Ol' Ryder. We gonna talk to him first. For your sake, hopefully last."

Ryder's heart went cold. Every gaze, save for that of Constance, turned to him. No one protested Corbin's demand.

"Just get to him," he whispered to Constance.

Ryder started forward. *Argo's silver,* he thought. *A story for kids.*

— ◆ —

It had been close. The little bastard Felix Hines came calling on the horses. Before hopping into the wagon, Felix looked at the canvas, scrutinizing it. He walked to the back of the wagon and raised the tarpaulin, probing the charnel house below. The kid's face was blank, emotionless. He was in his own world of obsession, absorbed.

Hector, fifteen feet away in the brush, prayed, finding a religion he'd abandoned since childhood. He made promises.

Felix was untroubled by what he saw beneath the tarp. He climbed to the buckboard and snapped at the horses. The animals flinched, then they started forward. Felix whistled a tune, "The Hunters of Kentucky." It was, Hector recognized, a melody Brigham Conway played on the fiddle at Rand's.

The strain of waiting was too much to bear. He did more praying.

As the wagon moved along the road, cresting the hill and then dropping out of sight, Hector began the grueling crawl. On hands and knees, he inched forward.

HE never told his father what he saw. He never told the deputy. No one pushed the boy to divulge the truth. A combination of fear and shame made him lock it away. The memory became morbid, eventually taboo. Elijah sent the pain deep into his mind.

His father left. The boy grew estranged. The last time he saw his old man was on the gallows, a canvas hood covering his head. There were no eyes in the hood.

A hangman waited on the scaffolding. The hangman's eyes found Elijah in the crowd. This was his moment of glory—a daub of color upon a field of stone.

The boy recognized something in the man's eyes.

Painfully, the memory of his mother surfaced. It was not the same face. This hangman was twenty years the junior of his mother's killer, but he shared the same look in his eyes. His eyes were old.

Elijah realized then that the Hangman wore a multitude of faces. The thought seared into his mind. He stood frozen with revelation.

The Hangman plied his trade.

While he did, Elijah Valero decided his fate.

THE men stood in shafts of sunlight, still enough that motes settled on their shoulders. The air smelled of stale beer and wood smoke. A group of huddled children cried softly. It was a pitiful assortment, bullies and blowhards, some yearning for a fortune, some desperate for isolation. To the last of them, they were cowards. Even Talbot and Thorn were cowards. They only stormed out the door because they couldn't stand waiting any longer. It was shameful that the men outside were allowed to take Ryder. No one attempted to stop them.

Constance had to find the strength of mind to be calm. Hector was gone. She only skimmed the surface of that thought, not daring to stare into the abyss of it. She was needed. Pierce relied on her. She could not fold beneath grief, at least not yet. The time for that would come. With monumental will, she dried her face and stood. She walked to one of the hazy windows and gazed out onto the street. Rand's was quiet. Of the men outside, she knew nothing. She recognized only the face of Felix Hines.

What could they possibly want with Pierce? What could he tell them? Everyone knew there was no truth about Argo's silver. It was a story that children told, but a legend that not even they believed. Perhaps the men wanted Pierce for cruelty alone. The stouter of the men, the one who so viciously hurt Talbot, held Pierce by the back of the neck. His massive hand reached around to the front of the old man's throat. Pierce's hat lay in the dirt.

The other man aimed a rifle at the windows. Felix held a long knife but appeared unmoved. Pierce had taught the child a great deal. Felix didn't convey that he even knew the man. The coldness frightened Constance. To the boy, even Pierce was only flesh and bone, soon to be dust.

With haste, Constance walked around the bar, avoiding eye contact with the children who sat atop it, and stepped into the back room that Brigham Conway used for living quarters. No one was here. It was a solemn room, with a small cot in the corner and a chest of drawers at one side. There was a mud-brown fiddle atop the chest, and there was a silver locket. In the center of the floor, concealed by a rug, there was a square door on two hinges. She kicked back the rug. The door, which led to a sizeable cellar, had an iron ring for a handle. Constance opened the door wide, and the must of earth billowed from the darkness. She knew of the cellar only because of Hector. Brigham used the hole as a holding tank for troublesome drunks.

A wooden ladder descended five feet to the dirt floor. She climbed down the first two rungs, then she hopped to the ground. She bent at the waist to fit into the cramped, cool darkness. A few barrels lined one of the walls. There was a squat shelf and glass bottles, a myriad of shapes, on another wall.

There had to be another way in and out other than the trap in the floor. Despite the low light, she gauged that the cellar extended ten feet in any direction. Over her right shoulder, she spotted a thin line of sunlight. The lines formed a rectangle. With an effort not to bust her head against the ceiling, she rushed towards the light. She felt for a handle in the darkness. When she found it, she pushed. The door was jammed in place or weighted on the other side. The specter of being locked in brought a feeling of claustrophobia. Constance willed herself not to panic.

Putting her shoulder against the door, she gave a tremendous shove. The door lifted a few inches and then fell with a bang. Her heart went cold. The noise might as well have been a gunshot. She shoved again, now harder, but the result was the same. The world seemed as though it would crash. She felt indescribably small. She thought of Hector. Tears stung her eyes. She listened, fearing footsteps outside. There were none.

Gathering herself, she devised another strategy. Placing her shoulder against the planks, Constance heaved slowly, as if rising to stand erect. Sunlight poured through the fissure. The door rose several inches, until her spine shook with the weight. After taking a deep breath and biting her tongue, she shoved her forearm through the opening. The weight bruised to the bone as she lowered it back onto her arm. She felt the mud outside and the sunlight. The door would not close again.

She put her shoulder against the wood once more, and then she lifted higher than she had previously. The effort created enough space for Constance to put her entire arm outside, up to the shoulder. Then, as the other shoulder maintained the weight, she stuck her head through. She gasped for air as the door came down on her back, but it was not enough to crush her. She saw what weighted the door. Atop the planks were several pails of crushed stone. She managed to tip one over and shove it off the door. Then she had both arms free. She toppled another and it rolled into the mud. She climbed until the door met her waist, and then she freed her legs.

From here, sitting in a patch of mud, she saw the railroad tracks and familiar depot. The sight ruined her resolve, and she sobbed. She and Hector were so close to leaving. Only a morning prior she had stood there and imagined. She cried harder, but she stood as she did. Her back and arms were sore with bruises. When she was positive she was alone, she mustered the grit that remained and sprinted into the woods.

———◆———

The cabin stood on a flat where the hill crested and where a ravine cut by cascading rainwater led to the river. The shelter was lopsided and rotten, having decayed at the left foundation. The shutters were askew on their hinges, and a sandstone chimney poked from the sagging roof. It had been years since the cabin was used for a purpose. Now forlorn, it would remain exposed to the elements until it fell in on itself.

Constance, numbed by the exertion, reached the field of weeds that led to the cabin's front door. She had sprinted the distance. She waded into grasses that reached as high as her waist, grasses infested with ticks and buzzing life.

On the front stoop, a dark figure reclined with his back against the door. He was rolling a cigarette methodically. Sophia, Pierce's dog, waited at the man's side. The dog was not a ball of energy like normal. Rather, she mirrored the man's stillness. Constance pushed through the last of the weeds, and she stopped as she entered the cabin's shadow. A chorus of insects surrounded her. She stood, breathing heavily, thoughts racing, gauging the man who sat before her. Sophia, oddly, did not greet her. The dog ignored Constance. Elijah Valero had somehow infected the animal.

Valero's eyes were wary. He looked up at Constance slowly, without commitment to seeing her, as if entranced by something in his mind's eye. His face was worn, a shade of leather marked with crow's feet and bags under his grey eyes. He wore a full beard, black as pitch, unkempt and nearly four inches long. He was too thin for his frame, his bones too prominent, as though he'd starved. Shaggy hair, dark as the beard, fell over his forehead and covered his ears. Above all else, the eyes drew Constance. There was something in them that pulled, a portentous air. Despite his appearance, he was no vagrant. As she stared, the man betrayed no emotion, save for the vaguest sense of hatred.

"We need your help," she began. "We'll give you anything."

Valero moved his shoulder, exposing the gun in his pocket, and Constance flinched. She couldn't help it. The man terrified her in the way a wild animal, an unpredictable thing, would terrify anyone. Valero noticed her revulsion, and his eyes reflected anything but pride. He said nothing. He put the cigarette in his mouth. He lit it with a match.

"They killed two—" She stopped then, the image of the wagon entering her mind. She tried to frame the words. "They killed everybody," she said lamely.

Valero reached over and stroked Sophia's ears. The dog cooed at his touch.

"Who?" Valero asked. Smoke seeped from the edge of his mouth. He cracked his neck, unconcerned.

"Felix Hines—"

"—The boy they were chasin'?" He smirked.

"That's him, yes. He's got two others with him. I'm not sure what their names are."

Valero nodded. He was unfazed. He took another drag on the cigarette.

"Isn't that enough? They killed Hector. They have Pierce right now."

For the first time, Valero showed emotion. It was simple, but he grimaced at the mention of Pierce Ryder. He flicked ashes into the dirt at his feet.

"What do they want?" he asked.

"They think there's silver hidden in town. They think Pierce will tell them where it's at."

Valero smirked again.

"Yeah, I noticed that. They should ask his dog, not him." Valero laughed, and it was a creepy, bizarre sound. It was disconnected from his humanity. He reached into his pocket and pulled out two silver coins, old coins. "That what they're lookin' for?" He gestured at Sophia with the cigarette. "She dug holes all night." He laughed again, and it was hollow.

"There is no silver," Constance said.

Valero shrugged. He put the coins away. "There's a gun crate of coins buried back that way." He motioned with a nod.

Constance grew frustrated.

"None of that matters. Will you help Pierce or not?" She moved on from "us" because that had no impact. Valero cared for the old man.

Valero stood. He worked on the cigarette more. He took such a long pause between speaking that it seemed he struggled to choose his words.

"I s'pose I will. I want that horse, though."

"What?"

"Take me to the stable."

Her frown was plaintive.

"Please don't hurt us," she said. "Please."

Elijah Valero showed emotion for the second time, and it was shame.

"Come on," he told Sophia. The dog stood at his command. "Let's go get your old man."

RYDER stepped through the saloon doors and into the light, thinking of Connie, praying she'd be able to get out without being noticed. In the street stood Felix, Corbin, and Spence. On the ground lay Thorn and Talbot. In the wagon and beyond it toward the shanties lay just about everybody else. As he stepped into mud, Ryder shrank with terror. He tried to make himself ready to die. Outwardly, he kept his stoicism. He was even conscious not to slouch, yet another trick he learned in the Army.

Spence greeted him with a roll of the shoulders. He nodded at Talbot's grotesque form, still prostrate.

"You don't want that to happen again, do you?"

Ryder avoided Spence's eyes. He looked instead at Felix. He wanted to find something human in the boy. Felix kept his bloodshot eyes forward, unbothered. Soot streaked his jaws.

Corbin stood to the side with a rifle aimed at Rand's. He said nothing.

"I'm gonna make this simple," Spence said. "You remember me, don't you?"

Ryder nodded.

The man spoke with an unusual rhythm, with a gait that suggested he overcame a stutter at some point in his life.

"You do remember that I, when we were in town to work, asked you about Old Man Argo?"

Again, Ryder nodded assent.

"That's good." Spence cracked his knuckles. "That pissant sheriff was nobody. I doubt he ever seen Argo. I'd say that goes for all the folks inside, too. Wouldn't you?"

Ryder didn't reply.

"Either you're friendly and answer, or we work you over."

"They don't know Argo."

"But you do. You know him damn well, I'd say. You run your mouth so much you let it slip to me that you was in the Army with him. That right?"

"Just get to it," Ryder said.

Spence grew stern. Whatever levity he possessed vanished.

"You're gonna tell us, and you're gonna show us, where that cache of silver is. Ain't that right?"

Ryder hesitated. As far as he knew, there was no silver. That was not going to be a satisfactory answer. It wouldn't fly with Spence Hickman. The man was too driven, too obsessed. Nothing could contradict the truth as he knew it. Ryder grew ill.

Spence read the hesitation incorrectly. He took it as affirmation; he took it as greed on the part of the old man. He took it as unwillingness.

"Here's what silence gets you." He looked at Corbin and Felix. "Go get one of 'em. Doesn't matter who."

Corbin kept his rifle aimed, but he started forward. Felix joined him.

"Until you talk, we drag 'em out one at a time. Little Felix has a machete and mallet on him. We won't even dignify 'em with a bullet. Understand? One at a time, all day and night if need be." He smiled. "I imagine that's mainly women and kids in there, ain't it? Hey, I bet the sheriff's wife's in there." Spence whistled. "I've been waitin' on that."

"Stop them," Ryder said.

"Talk."

"I'll show you where it is."

If nothing else, he could stall. He thought about Connie and Elijah, although his hope that they'd arrive in time to make a difference was dimming.

"How much is it?"

"More than the three of you could carry." Ryder swallowed, attempting to control the tremor in his voice. "You'll be satisfied."

Spence winked at Ryder. "Corby, pal, it's 'bout pay-day," he shouted. "Felix, get the horses ready." Then to Ryder, "Where?"

"There's a Spanish monastery about two hours ride from here," Ryder began.

"I knew it," Spence said. "Goddamn if I didn't know it." He looked at Ryder. "How much is it?" he asked again.

Ryder looked around at Rand's, and he looked at the hills beyond town. He saw no sign of Connie or Valero.

WHEN Valero, Sophia, and Constance reached town, the air was still, the men gone. Valero walked into the open street with the dog at his heels. Women and children filed out of Rand's Hotel. They stood slack-jawed, observing the carnage. A body lay on the hotel porch. An aura of dread and indignation hung in the air. Voices, too, hung in the air, uttering empty threats: would have, if only.

Valero battled his thoughts. Although he told her she was not real, that he was sick, the Spider's voice remained a prevalent one, as she had through the morning. Her words amounted to chatter, broken like a wave against the shore, but there was a central message in the tangle, and the message was self-preservation.

This is not your fight. A beautiful woman beguiled you. The old man beguiled you. When you've finished what they want, will they not don the Hangman's hood?

A volley of stinging insults peppered the chatter.

To face her and deny her was his only defense.

She isn't real. She isn't real. She isn't real.

Her message, however, was one that he was inclined to believe. It was a message he wanted to believe. But, unlike in the past, Valero moved forward anyway.

The crowd did not attempt to stop him. Maybe, in that moment, the survivors in Bone-of-Wellington wanted to reach out and make a deal with the Devil. Regardless of motivation, the people made no effort to confront him as he walked past Rand's.

"They took Pierce," a woman shouted to Constance. "All of 'em rode that way." She pointed at the road that led to the monastery.

The only figure that moved from the crowd was Wiley. He sprinted towards the livery as Valero approached. The boy had his finger on Valero's pulse.

"I'll get you whatever you need," he said. "I knew those men were tryin' to get a rise outta you. I told 'em so. I told 'em what I saw. I told 'em how fast you were, too. I told 'em again just now."

Valero ignored him. He moved into the shadowed interior, away from the sun, leaving Constance at the doorway. She offered no sage wisdom, no inane comparisons to her husband. For that restraint, Valero was glad.

The scent of straw surrounded him. He walked to the back stall. His heart quickened with anticipation.

"I'll get her saddled," Wiley said.

He knew. Did Maureen know?

The boy ran ahead with gear in his arms. He opened Maureen's stall and dashed inside.

"We got faster horses," Wiley said. "A hell of a lot faster."

"I'd rather have an angry one," Valero said.

He knelt and scratched Sophia's ears. The dog watched him, worried about his energy, as if she knew he were leaving.

"You're gonna stay with Mrs. Bray," he said. "You understand?"

Sophia rolled on her back, exposing her belly.

When Wiley finished, Valero mounted the roan. Sophia got to her feet and stepped aside. Valero leaned forward in the shadow, drawing his beard close to the horse's mane. Maureen shifted her shoulders.

"Run 'em down," Valero whispered.

Maureen lurched forward, beating the ground towards the sun-baked street. She moved with energy not even Valero knew she possessed. She dashed through the crowd, gaining the stage road, huffing from deep in her gut.

She knew.

For the first thirty yards, Sophia followed, pushing as hard as her short legs allowed. It was futile, though, and the dog dropped with grief when Valero was no longer in sight.

Constance ran after the dog.

CONSTANCE stood at the side of the road as Elijah, doubled at the waist and riding hard, thundered away. He was gone in a cloud of dust. Watching him brought mixed feelings. She had to breathe and rest, regain herself.

Sophia quit her pursuit, heartbroken. She slowed to a trot and then watched Valero fade. Ignoring Constance, the dog started back towards town, back towards Pierce's shack. Constance didn't attempt to rein her in.

It was then, while watching slumped Sophia retreat, that Constance heard his voice. It was an unmistakable sound. The world stopped. The voice was too vivid to be imagined. Constance looked about, searching the edge of the forest. She clenched her teeth, allowing hope to rise, and she listened.

"Connie," the voice repeated.

She saw him then.

Hector reached for a tree, pulling himself closer, dragging his body from the bramble. He looked up, his expression that of a stone-faced ghost.

The sight of his broken form shattered the dam of her grit. Constance ran to her husband, exhilarated, sobbing, bewildered by the raging emotions. She dropped to her knees when she reached him.

Hector, too, was crying.

"It was Felix. He brought two men."

Gasps punctuated his words. His eyes were clouded, as if a film lay over them. He was near death. He smelled of rot.

"I know," Constance said. She cradled his head. His skin was hot with fever. She looked with horror at the green and black wound at his ribs. His boots were gone, and his left foot had a tear as wide as an open mouth.

"They killed...."

"You don't have to talk," Constance said. She begged him to be still, to conserve his energy. She stroked his wet hair in a banal effort to calm him. "You're alive. That's all that matters."

Hector closed his eyes. He breathed steadily for several seconds before asking, "The town?"

Constance looked at the broken man, and his strength, his concern, made her proud. Shame washed over her.

"Everything's fine," she lied. "We have a man after them. He's a killer like them."

Hector opened his eyes, and a moment of clarity shone through.

"Valero," he said. It wasn't a question. He knew.

Constance nodded.

"You're safe," she said. "You're safe now."

FOURTEEN

ONLY when she reached the hill that sloped towards the monastery did Maureen slow her pace. Valero eased the horse to a stop. She sweated profusely and breathed from her gut, but her gait was strong, her back straight and proud, her tail erect. Valero patted her neck, and then he dismounted. Dust rose along the dirt trace.

Maureen snorted and shook her mane.

"Little Miss," Valero said. He adjusted her saddle. "Rest and wait down here. I'll be back when it's done."

He tied the mare's reins around the trunk of a baby sycamore. She stood in shade, off the road, out of sight from the monastery above. Her large tongue moved over her lips.

Valero prepared himself. His mind was clear. He thought about Pierce Ryder, and he thought about what he'd ask in return for this duty. The horse, yes, but also some silver. He could exact a hefty sum, but he'd settle for a few handfuls. He hadn't lied to Constance. There were chests of coins buried near the loggers' cabin. All the trouble these bastards were going through to find the silver, and a dog had uncovered it on a whim. Valero enjoyed that.

It was then that a voice came to him. It rang clearly through the trees, arrogant, careless, unafraid. Whoever it was believed they had the world by the neck. A predator without fear of predators.

"Goddamnit, I heard you," he shouted. There was verve in his voice, excitement. "I'm going. I'm looking."

Valero moved to Maureen's side once more. He petted her mane to keep her calm. Her breath was too loud to conceal, but it didn't matter. He simply didn't want her to buck and bend the tree, trying to run.

Footsteps, equally careless, followed the voice.

That's it, Valero thought, hearing the approach. *Come down here. Make it easy.*

Valero backed away from the horse, positioning himself in the shadow of the underbrush. He considered the gun but left his hands free. He recognized the voice as that of Felix Hines. He'd heard it before in the solarium.

Felix sauntered down the trail, playfully swinging a machete in his grip. He was a frail kid, pale and slender. He was so pleased with himself, he might as well have been whistling. He finished shouting to the men above, and he spoke to himself.

"I told you there wasn't—"

He stopped in the road. His demeanor changed when Maureen caught his eye. He furrowed his brow, and the machete dropped to his side, dangling. His features shrank.

Valero stayed in shadow. With calmness, he watched.

"What the hell are you doing here?" Felix said to the horse. He looked around, cutting a circle in the dirt. A fervid energy came off him. "Who brought you up here?"

When Valero sensed that the kid was poised to panic and run back to the monastery, he stepped out of the shade, making himself known.

Felix stared at the man before him, dumbfounded.

"Are you Felix Hines?" Valero asked.

Felix shook his head.

"Who the hell are you?"

Valero walked closer. He was prepared to spring after the kid if necessary.

Felix remained still. He brought up the machete as defense. He wore a gun in his waistband, but it was an afterthought. He didn't appear like he knew how to use a gun. Another knife, smaller, sheathed, hung at his side. The knife belonged to Pierce Ryder.

"Do you recognize that horse?" Valero asked.

He looked at Felix closely for the first time. He wasn't impressive. He looked weak in every sense. His mind was lost somewhere in his bloodshot eyes. There was nothing brave about him, either—he was a ball of nerves, a frightened pup. The way he held the machete was comical.

"Stay back," Felix said. He gestured with the blade.

"Do you or not?" Valero asked. "'Cuz she sure knows you."

"You the one who stole her?" Felix asked. His voice shook. Nerves took him apart rather than brought him together.

Valero nodded.

"Right up there," he said. He pointed. "You like beatin' on horses?"

"It's my horse. I can do what I want to it."

"That's all I needed to hear," Valero said.

Felix brought up the machete, cocking it as if to strike. He brandished the weapon like a hatchet. Pathetic animal that he was, it made for an absurd sight.

"Get a good look at her," Valero said.

Felix swung.

Valero didn't draw his gun—he didn't want the attention the explosion would bring, not yet. He ducked to the side, avoiding the blade, and he grabbed the kid's arm with two hands. The swing stopped, and the machete remained high in the air. Gripping at the wrist and elbow, Valero brought the arm down hard against his rising knee. The connection was clean. His forearm snapped with a pop. Felix screamed, and the machete fell to the dirt.

If there'd ever been any fight in the kid, the agony took it out of him. His face was white with shock.

Still gripping the cracked arm, Valero grabbed higher towards the shoulder and swung Felix to the ground. He kept the wrist in his grip so the pressure on the broken arm wouldn't lessen. Felix had no weight. He struck the ground with this free shoulder. His only resistance was to roll on his back, kicking like a trapped dog. He didn't go for the gun or knife at his waist. He didn't do anything except shake at the mouth and cry out.

Valero stepped on his neck to quiet him. It was a long, thin neck, exposed. He let his weight mash the kid's throat. The passageways closed. The screaming stopped.

Felix went red and then purple.

With his boot in place, Valero dropped Felix's wrist. The slender arm fell lifelessly. The flesh grew purple. Valero knelt, coming so near that Felix could hear a whisper.

Felix tried to shout, but nothing but a groan escaped. His tongue appeared to swell in his mouth, filling it. Lines of green moved through the purple under his skin.

"Is Ryder up there with the others?" Valero asked.

A bone, brittle as the snap of an icicle, cracked in Felix's throat.

Valero grimaced. That was that. There'd be no answer. He meant to control his weight, but it had been a while since he'd stepped on a man's neck.

He pulled the knife from Felix's waistband. It was a simple tool, a blade Ryder used for carving. It was no more than four inches long.

Valero pressed harder with the boot until Felix's eyes bulged. No breath went in or came out. His skin turned a mottled purple. The hue deepened. Thick veins showed on his forehead and around his eyes. Felix kicked at the dirt, drawing lines with the heels of his boots.

Valero glanced at Maureen.

He brought the knife down hard against Felix's gut. The blade entered to the edge of Valero's hand without resistance.

Felix bucked and kicked harder, but he was unable to make a sound.

Valero pulled the blade free and admired the streak of blood on it. He allowed Felix to see it. Blood pulsed from the wound, wetting Felix's shirt. Valero punched the knife down again. Then again. He stabbed Felix ten times, tearing open his gut, before he stopped.

The kid went quietly. When he stopped kicking, shaking, and pissing, he was dead.

Somebody should've done that to you a long time ago, Valero thought.

He stood with the knife. The steel was bloody, as was his hand. He returned to the horse that way. With his thumb, Valero wiped blood on Maureen's snout. The rest he wiped on his trousers. He threw the blade into a bank of weeds. Ryder wouldn't want it.

Valero watched Felix as he started toward the monastery. The kid's mouth was open impossibly wide, framing a scream that didn't emerge. The grid of veins on his face resembled a spiderweb.

THE top edge of the monastery rose above the trees—bleached stone that led downward to moss and vine, downward into a rotten vestibule. Valero felt an aversion to the ruins. He couldn't separate the image from shame. He fought the urge to remember by checking his Colt. The gun was loaded.

Three horses stood outside the front wall. One was a Morgan filched from Wiley's stable. The horses waited with saddle and bridle, solemn in the brown grass. Beyond the wall stood the monastery. The windows were dark, the mullioned solarium without movement. The rankness of death and vermin emanated from the garden.

Valero sprinted to the wall. He stopped and crouched, waiting for a voice or gunshot, any effort to halt his approach. He waited, but he heard nothing that mattered. Birdsong and the chatter of insects came to him, nothing more. Steeling himself, he peered around stone into the garden.

Old blood, pieces of clothing, and other debris lay strewn across the mashed weeds. In the middle of the garden was a fire pit with a man's face buried in the ashes. His body lay beside the fire like the raised tail of a smashed mouse. His clothes were charred. Another corpse, fatter and missing its head, lay near the gate. One of the hands clutched dirt. Flies and wasps swarmed the body, thick as bees undulating in a hive.

These were, Valero assumed, the remnants of the posse he'd encountered on the road. They'd ridden directly into a massacre. A thought of the peace officer, Hector with his clean vest, flashed in his mind. Valero pitied Constance Bray. Such brutality was an undeserved fate. Knowledge of this scene would render her fragile as glass.

The woman was with child, too.

Valero's thoughts returned to the conversation at Ryder's.

Is Hector a righteous man?

Constance said no, but only a righteous man was fool enough to take on such a burden when he had a wife and child to look after.

Satisfied that no one gave a damn about Felix's absence, Valero repeated his careful approach until he had a foothold in the breezeway. He hurried along the trail of corpses. Either by apathy or design, no one shot at him. Once in the solarium, Valero was able to walk the monastery from edge to edge, but the walk would leave him exposed. He had to get inside for cover.

They're busy with Ryder, he reasoned.

Or they tempt your foolishness, another voice suggested. *They feed your arrogance.*

Valero shut his eyes and breathed.

Or that, he thought.

Making himself thin against the wall, he listened for movement. Valero pulled the revolver from his pocket once more. He cocked the hammer. He moved towards the main entrance, the door with the stairwell immediately beyond. He had the idea of getting upstairs. As he neared the opening, Valero caught a faint melody, one he recognized.

Dig a grave, dig a grave in the meadow
Dig a grave in the cold hard ground

It was not a memory. The melody was not a phantom. A man approached, plodding down the stairs without grace, and he whistled the tune.

They beguile you, the Spider said. *Why help them? Why help when they want nothing but to watch you die?*

Valero steadied his Colt, holding the gun firmly at his waist. He stepped back from the doorway.

The whistling stopped clean, as did the man, when he emerged from the shadowed interior. He was a tall man, ghastly thin, with a dead eye in his face. He carried a rifle in one hand. If he were surprised, he didn't allow the expression to register. He looked down at Valero's gun and grinned. His front teeth were gone. Valero recognized the man from the watering hole.

The man recognized Valero, too.

"If it ain't the graveyard ghost," he said, still grinning. "I'll be damned. What's a fuckin' tramp like you doin' up here?"

Valero motioned with the gun for the man to step fully into the open.

The man obliged.

"What'd you do with the kid?" he asked.

Valero watched the man, and he looked around him for a sign of the other. For now, they were alone. Wind moved through the garden, carrying the aroma of charred meat and the thrumming of insects. Valero's eyes fell on the rifle.

"Put it on the ground," he said.

The man shrugged. He placed the rifle on the stone floor.

"Ain't nothin'," he said. "What'd you do with the fuckin' kid?"

"Where's Ryder?" Valero asked.

"That puts us at odds, don't it? Shit, you know I told Spence I recognized you. Can't put a finger on it, though. What's your name, graveyard ghost?"

"Tell me where the old man is."

"Hell, you got me. I'm done. Least you can do is tell me your fuckin' name. You prob'ly fucked up that kid good, didn't you?" He shook his head. He put his hands in the air, a half-hearted gesture of surrender. "You go first."

"Eli Valero."

The man's grin straightened.

"You're fuckin' with me." He shook his head. "Nah. Ain't no way."

"You're gonna take me to Ryder or you're gonna die right here."

"What if he's dead? What then, Mr. Valero?" The man laughed. "You know, I saw Eli Valero get paid cold hard cash to shoot a German in the fuckin' head. He did it, too. Years ago. That's you, huh? You look down on your luck. Starved like a mangy fuckin' mutt. Who's payin' you now?"

Valero pulled a few coins from his pocket.

"They got more silver than they know what to do with," he taunted.

He flipped one of the coins. It hit the man in the chest and fell to the ground. The coin rolled into the weeds.

The man's demeanor changed. He swallowed, and a large Adam's apple bobbed in his gaunt throat.

"Where'd you get that?"

"Not up here," Valero said. "There's whole chests of it. You wouldn't believe it, but you ain't even close."

The man pointed a bony finger.

"You're fuckin' lyin'," he said. "That old man's lead-in' Spence to the silver right now. Ryder pay you? He give you those fuckin' coins?"

"You got one more chance. Where's Ryder?"

Color crept into the man's features. A slash of red crossed his jaws.

"He took Spence down into the cellar."

"Show me."

A shotgun snapped behind him, and Valero knew instantly he'd made a fatal mistake. He'd allowed the man to keep talking. He'd allowed him to stall.

"Corbin, who the hell is this bastard? Gun down, boy."

Valero turned to see the barrel pointed at his head. He loosened his grip on the Colt. He lowered the hammer.

The Spider whispered memories, taunting.

Is your loyalty to me so fragile? Did I not protect you? All these years, did I not help you to see?

Where is the rider? Where is the noose?

The Hangman is come again, Elijah. He ensnared you.

Corbin regained his composure. He spoke as if he never lost it, as though he'd been in control all along.

"Hey, now. You better watch it. That's goddamn Eli Valero standin' before you."

Valero looked at the man with the shotgun. He was stout, built like a bull, and hard as hell. Unlike his partner, there was nothing sardonic in his face. He found humor in scraping off skin on a grindstone. He stood alone. Ryder was nowhere in sight.

"If that's Eli Valero, he don't really live up to his image, does he? I heard you was a lunatic."

Valero stood firm, staring.

The Spider taunted but offered no guidance.

"The swimmin' hole," the bull said. "That's where I seen you. I've wanted to beat your ass ever since."

"Open him up, Spence. He's got silver inside."

Spence looked at Corbin.

"You serious?"

"Yeah, he's fuckin' braggin' about it." Corbin pointed at the coin at the edge of the weeds. "He says Ryder's lyin'. He says it ain't up here."

Spence shook his head.

"Gun down," he repeated.

Valero placed the Colt on the ground.

"I'm gonna fuck that old man up his ass with this shotgun until he dies. Swear to God." Spence watched Valero, searching his eyes. "Where's it at? If it ain't here, where is it?"

"'Bout as far from here as you can get," Valero said. "You went the wrong way."

Spence scratched his mustache. He didn't hide his frustration.

"Get those guns off the ground, Corby. Keep that Colt. If this is Valero, we'll sell the shit outta that." He looked Valero up and down. "I might cut you up and sell you in pieces. You wanna show me where that silver's at or you gonna make me work on you?"

With delicacy, Valero took another coin from his pocket. He flipped it across the divide—it landed at Spence's boot.

Spence motioned for Corbin to join him.

"Take this," he said. He handed over the shotgun and a pistol from his belt. "You either show me or I make you show me. Maybe you saw what it took to get the old man to cooperate. What'll it take with you? You look a little frail."

Valero stared.

Spence nodded.

"Your turn then. I'm gonna take you apart."

"Get 'em, boy." Corbin laughed. He backed away with the guns.

Spence moved like a bareknuckle boxer, without telegraphing his direction or punches. Before Valero stepped back, Spence dipped and rammed him in the gut, driving him to the ground with his shoulder. Valero's back struck hard against stone. The blow knocked the wind out of him, and he gasped.

Spence moved fast. He smashed Valero's thigh with one knee, planted the other, and then started pummeling, hammering with blows that began in his thick shoulders.

Valero struggled, throwing his arms over his face to deflect the worst of the strikes. He tried to roll out from beneath Spence's weight, but he didn't manage it. Spence showed no sign of tiring. The punches were rapid and fast, relentless. One swing after another for nearly thirty seconds.

Although he sacrificed his face to do so, suffering a smashed nose that shot blood over his eyes, Valero managed to hook Spence's leg. He couldn't throw the man aside, but he upset his balance. The punches stopped momentarily. Valero kicked Spence back and freed himself.

Valero sat on the ground, his face throbbing and bloody, a whistle in his ear like a scream.

"With a gun," he said. He breathed heavily.

Spence, sweat pouring at his temples, wetting his hair, smiled. He was on his knees. He laughed.

"Is that how'd like it? You're a killer, huh?"

Valero's rage built.

"With a gun," he repeated. He wiped blood from his face.

Spence cracked his neck and stood.

"You got it," he said. He looked at Corbin. "Give him his gun."

"You fuckin' asshole. You kiddin' me?"

Spence glared.

"If that's Valero, I'm gonna kill him right. Give him his gun. Gimme back that pistol."

Corbin threw the Colt on the ground. He returned the pistol to Spence.

Valero looked at the gun. In his condition, he couldn't beat Spence with his fists. He had to do it the way he knew best.

Valero leapt for the gun. Spence was lifting his pistol, readying it, when the first shot exploded from the Colt's octagonal barrel. The blast shrieked through the ruins.

A bullet tore open Spence's stomach and studded the wall, kicking dust from stone. Spence staggered but didn't fall. His face went red. Veins tightened in his neck. He managed to keep his grasp on the pistol.

Valero stood, blood streaming over his mouth and into his beard. He fired again, calmer, more assured, and a spray of blood jetted from the side of Spence's skull. The bull had a look of rage even when he went to his knees.

"You forgot your game," Valero said.

The life had gone from Spence, but the anger remained, like it was etched in granite. Unconscious, he fell to his back and bled out. He died properly, with his skull opened.

Valero looked around. He stepped on Spence's wrist, crunching bone. He turned the Colt.

Corbin stood back from the action, slack-jawed. He held the rifle and shotgun like walking sticks.

"Goddamn if you ain't fuckin' Valero," he said. He looked down at the rifle. "Hell, I was only fuckin' around, man. I ain't even—"

Valero aimed the Colt.

"Take me to Ryder," he said.

Voluntarily, Corbin put the rifle and shotgun on the ground.

"Move," Valero said. He wiped blood from his mouth.

Corbin nodded. He started down the solarium.

"He's in that big church room down here." His voice shook. He had trouble framing the words.

"Did you hurt him?"

"Well, I mean ... Not too bad." Corbin laughed nervously. He stopped and turned. "You really find that silver or you just fuckin' with me?"

"Move," Valero said.

"I gotta know." Corbin stuck his hand out. "Swear to God, I ain't—"

Valero pulled the trigger, blowing off the pinky and ring finger on Corbin's right hand. The man screamed out and went to his knees. His mutilated hand went to his chest, a fetal coil, smothering the blood flow. His fingers lay beside him on the ground.

Pathetically, slowly, Corbin went for a blade in his pocket. He got the knife free, but he didn't manage to throw it.

Valero put a bullet in his left hand, ripping open the palm.

The knife skidded across the stone floor.

Corbin fell on his back. He writhed and cried out.

"Move. Crawl if you have to," Valero said.

Through tears, Corbin said, "You sonnuva bitch, what the fuck did I ever do to you?"

Valero considered the question, but he didn't humor the man with a response. *You're the Hangman,* he thought, satisfied.

The Spider offered no resistance to this revelation.

"Get to your feet," Valero said.

Shakily, Corbin stood. Blood poured from his hands, dropping in gobs to the stone. He left a trail as he walked. He shuffled until he reached the chapel door. Corbin looked at Valero, his mouth open, his face sodden with sweat and tears.

Valero stepped into the large, airy room, full of must. He pushed Corbin ahead.

"How you gonna kill me?" Corbin asked.

"Ryder's dead, isn't he?"

Corbin searched the room with his working eye. Keeping both hands against his chest, pressing them to lessen the pain, he let out a choked sob.

"He's up on that front bench."

Valero shoved Corbin forward.

They walked down the aisle towards the front of the pews.

In the first row, lying on his back with rope coiled on his chest, was Pierce Ryder. His crumpled hat was missing. Dried blood covered his forehead. He was very small, very fragile. One of his legs was bent at the knee and tucked beneath him.

"Spence hit him too hard," Corbin said.

"Get on the ground," Valero ordered.

"I ain't—"

"On your knees."

"I ain't sure he's dead."

Corbin got on his knees, facing the altar.

Valero moved behind him, flipped the Colt, gripped the barrel, and brought down the handle against Corbin's skull. The first blow put him on the ground. The second left him unconscious but breathing. Valero considered a third, but the idea of the rope took hold.

Hang him, the Spider said. *Hang the Hangman. Leave him here. Let him feed the jackals.*

Hang the old man, as well. He'll betray you once he is safe.

As Valero approached Ryder, he saw subtle movement in the man's chest. He was breathing, albeit lightly. Valero put his fingers against the man's throat. He had a strong pulse.

Hang him while he's weak, the Spider said. *Rid yourself of the burden.*

Valero lifted the rope, straightened it on the pew, and he began to fashion a noose.

VALERO walked Maureen through the solarium, searching for a puddle of water. When they came upon Spence's prostrate form, Maureen stopped. The man's skull had a hole above the left ear. Brain matted his hair, and blood marked the stone where he fell. His eyes and mouth were open.

Out of curiosity, Maureen's snout inched closer to Spence's gaping maw. She snorted at the vile mess.

Valero scratched her mane.

"You got the belly for it," he said.

Nervous, the horse stepped back, shaking her head.

An abomination crawled from Spence's mouth.

Valero stepped back with the horse.

The Spider pressed against Spence's lip, emerging incarnate. It walked along his chin, down his neck, and then scuttled onto the stone. The Spider was massive. Black hair covered the legs.

Valero and the horse saw the arachnid, but only Valero heard the voice.

The old man, the Spider said. *He rode to town without you. He'll bring men back to capture you. Then what, Elijah? What will you do? You know where the silver is, and they do not.*

As Valero watched, the Spider walked around the contour of Spence's knee. The legs grew longer. He had no interest in seeing how large she could grow. Horror wrapped his spine.

Valero did something he had never done. In a fit of rage, he stomped the Spider, crushing her against stone.

She did not protest the action. She did not attempt to avoid it. When it was through, when her body was broken, she was silent.

Alarmed, Maureen pulled. Valero held her reins tightly. He scratched her neck until she calmed.

"There'll be no more of that," he whispered.

Is that a promise? he thought. *He considered, and he watched the smear on the ground. I'll leave you here. You and Spence can haunt the ruins.*

"Come along," Valero told the horse. He pulled her past the corpse and the Spider, and he didn't turn back.

When he and Maureen reached Pierce Ryder, the old man had finally opened his eyes. He was outside the chapel, propped in the shade against the wall. The day was getting on, and it was hot. Sweat dotted his swollen face.

Valero relinquished his grip on the horse's reins. She peered around her hindquarters, but the mare remained at Valero's side.

As the original builders had intended, birdsong moved through the breezeway. The peaceful sound contrasted starkly with the horrors of the garden and chapel.

Ryder looked up, sick in the eyes, groggy, concussed. Pain didn't mask the underlying joy of the moment, however. He attempted a smile.

"What happened?" he asked. His verve, his presence, was absent from the curiosity. The effort made him ill.

"You're gonna make it, old man," Valero said. "But you gotta relax. I'm gonna get you back home before dark."

"Connie reached you." That pleased Ryder. "I knew she could do it. She's strong, Elijah." He paused. "What happened to Felix?"

Valero shook his head.

"Corbin and Spence?"

"They won't give you any trouble," Valero said.

Gingerly, Ryder checked the wound on his forehead. He winced. The bruise was so large, it looked like Spence had cracked his head against a pew. The skin was split.

"They smashed up your face pretty good," Ryder said. "That's a broken nose. You feelin' okay? If you're anything like me, it hurts to goddamn breathe."

Valero shrugged. The crushed nose had swollen shut one of his eyes.

Ryder reclined his head. "All this was over silver that doesn't exist. Did Connie tell you that?"

The corner of Valero's mouth lifted with a smile. He pulled another coin from his pocket.

"There you're wrong, old man."

He flipped the coin into Ryder's lap.

Confused, Ryder grabbed the piece of silver. He ran it under his thumb, examining it. He looked up.

"There's a whole hell of a lot more," Valero said. "Chests of it."

"Where'd you find that?" Ryder asked. He had a wry look, as if he and Valero shared a joke.

"Ask your dog," Valero said. "She's the one that found it. Come on now. Get up."

"Sophia found it?"

Valero helped Ryder to his feet. The old man stood on shaky legs, but he had enough grit to ride.

"You tellin' me there's silver buried here? Those assholes were right all along?"

"They were right," Valero said.

"That son of a bitch Argo."

Ryder turned to the chapel entrance, but Valero stopped him.

"You don't wanna be in there," Valero said. "You've seen enough."

"My hat," Ryder said.

"Your hat's waitin' with the horses. I already got it. Come on before it gets dark."

Ryder turned his back to the chapel.

He didn't see the shadow on the ground. He didn't see the long form of Corbin Blum hanging by the neck from a rafter, swaying with the breeze, an old rope and rotten wood creaking with his weight. He didn't see Felix Hines' corpse propped against the altar.

Valero checked inside. He admired Corbin, and he was satisfied.

Once in the garden, Ryder averted his eyes from the carnage. He limped along.

Valero pulled Maureen. The horse was tired, so he planned to ride one of the other horses and string her along.

"I can't begin to thank you," Ryder started.

Valero retrieved Spence's shotgun from Maureen's side. He handed it to Ryder to use as a crutch.

Ryder took the gun.

"I'll tell you how you're gonna thank me," Valero said. "I'm takin' this horse. I'm takin' as much silver as I can carry. And nobody's gonna follow me when I go. Is that good enough?"

As if he had a choice, Ryder agreed. He reached for the kepi that wasn't there, an anxious gesture.

"That son of a bitch Argo," he repeated. "I guess it wouldn't do to ask you to stick around and shoot him, too."

Valero pulled a couple cigarettes from his pocket. He lit both. He gave one to Ryder.

"No," he said. "It wouldn't do."

Ryder drew on the cigarette greedily.

"Will you tell me somethin'?" he asked, exhaling. "What'd Connie say to convince you?"

Valero looked at the old man. He blew a cloud of smoke from the corner of his mouth.

When they approached the milling horses, Valero finally replied.

"It wasn't anything she said."

"What then?"

"I had to get you home to that pup, didn't I? She'd be up here, too, if her legs could handle it."

Ryder smiled. "You did it for the dog and not for me."

"That's right."

Valero selected the Morgan for Ryder. He guided the old man into the stirrup, and then he gave a push to get him over the horse's back.

"Because you like animals," said Ryder, looking down.

"You got a good memory, old man. Hold tight now. You're still loopy."

CONSTANCE put her arm around Hector, assisting him up the stairs to the depot platform.

"I'm the one who needs help," she teased.

Hector smiled at her swollen belly. She was six months pregnant.

Pierce Ryder came walking around the side of Rand's Hotel. With the train close, he carried Sophia. He was waving.

Once on the flat planks, Constance gave Hector his cane. He released his hold on her shoulder, and he leaned on the simple crutch. It did her heart good to see him standing again, even with assistance. Hector had been bedridden for so many months that it took its toll on both of them. He was morose and depressed. He experienced terrible nightmares from which he awoke with a start. Hector, despite prodding, would not divulge the content of the dreams, but the look in his eyes was enough to horrify Constance.

Sometimes his talk was poisonous, sometimes grandiose, but he never spoke of Felix, Corbin, Spence, or Valero.

Hector wasn't the same, but neither was Constance.

Ryder joined the couple on the depot. He grinned at Constance. He put his hand on Hector's shoulder.

"How you feelin'?" he asked.

Hector frowned, but he couldn't put his feelings into words. He had developed resentment for such questions.

As Sophia squirmed in his grasp, Ryder pulled a bag from his jacket. He handed the pouch to Constance.

"What's this?" she asked.

Holding it, weighing it in the hand, made the answer obvious. The bag was heavy with silver coins.

Ryder watched Hector for a reaction, but he received none.

"Call it a pension," he said. "Or severance. Or whatever the hell you like."

Constance's face reddened. She couldn't think of the way things had been. She pushed down the feelings, not allowing the memories to surface.

It's theft, she thought, but she knew how Pierce would reply.

I'm the one doing the thieving, he'd say. He'd said it before.

She hugged Pierce.

Tears brimmed in the old man's eyes.

This was not how Constance imagined her scene of departure.

Bone-of-Wellington was on the verge of abandonment. The graveyard was full, and workers had departed in droves. Only a handful of men remained. Even the whores had gone. Winter would be harsh and lonely, but Pierce was determined to stay behind. He'd be the last man to leave.

Winter would be a season for bountiful snow. Even now there were flurries in the air. Heavy clouds masked the sun, casting the surrounding hills grey. Summer had passed. Fall had passed. Trains came and went, came and went.

Of the silver, Old Man Argo was left with next to nothing. Elijah Valero departed with an enormous share. The Brays had a share. Ryder and Sophia hoarded a share. One chest remained behind the old cabin, undisturbed.

In the distance, the whistle of a locomotive sounded, passing over the river and through the cold, muddy streets.

Constance took Hector's hand and squeezed it.

"It's finally here," she said. "California."

Hector didn't speak as often as he once had, but he smiled again.

At a monastery in the wilderness, where snow fell harder, accumulated quicker, and lasted longer, all was silent. In the chapel, snow trickled through holes in the tall ceiling and drifted to the pews. Snow fell over a corpse resting at the foot of the altar, and snow gathered on the broken rope and coiled form of a hanged man now fallen to the floor. The rope had snapped months prior. Coyotes had vandalized, rearranged, and stripped the remains. Corbin was nude sinew attached to a tuft of hair. Felix's outstretched leg was reduced to bone. His face was chewed and rotten.

No visitors broke the spell of the scene. Even the chatter of rats was absent. The colony had, for the winter months, retreated through a hole in the kitchen floor to the cellar where there was neither wind nor snow. The rats nested, and their store of food was more plentiful than it had been in years.

Elijah Valero was five hundred miles from Bone-of-Wellington. He sat in a hotel room, atop a straw bed, listening to a voice in the darkness.

A NOTE ON THE TYPE

The text of this book is set in Freight Text Pro, a serif typeface designed by Joshua Darden in 2005 for the Brooklyn based Darden Studio type foundry.

Joshua Darden was born and raised in suburban Los Angeles. Joshua published his first typeface at the age of 15. He spent the next ten years of his life as an assistant for typeface development and worked for a wide range of commercial clients. Darden worked briefly with other famous designers like David Carson. His Brooklyn based studio was established in 2004 and since then he has had the opportunity to be a guest lecturer and type critic for a number of colleges and art schools across the nation. Joshua Darden has also taught at Parsons School of Design and the School of Visual Arts.

Composed by Clever Crow Consulting and Design,
Pittsburgh, Pennsylvania

ABOUT THE AUTHOR

Coy Hall lives in West Virginia with his wife, and they share a home with their clumsy Great Pyrenees. Coy splits time as an author of horror and professor of history. History guides his writing, with most of his stories set in the past—sometimes the real past, sometimes an imagined one, but most often a mix of the two. Find out more about his stories and novels at www.coyhall.com.

NOSETOUCH PRESS

Nosetouch Press is an independent book publisher
tandemly based in Chicago and Pittsburgh.
We are dedicated to bringing some of today's most
energizing fiction to readers around the world.

Our commitment to classic book design in a digital
environment brings an innovative and authentic
approach to the traditions of literary excellence.

*We're Out There

NOSETOUCHPRESS.COM

Horror | Science Fiction | Fantasy | Mystery
Supernatural | Folk Horror | Occult | Gothic | Weird

Available in

HARDCOVER | PAPERBACK | EBOOK

NosetouchPress.com

Available in

HARDCOVER | PAPERBACK | EBOOK

NosetouchPress.com